BROKEN MANACLES

Mr Manas Manumohan

"The acts of the human race have doubtless a coherent unity, but the meaning of the vast tragedy enacted will be visible only to the Eye of God, until the end, which will reveal perhaps to the last man." - *Alfred De Vigny*

PROLOGUE

August 1651

"Who are *you*?" The question shook fear into the old, shaken man thinking of all the dimensions of that question. *Such a simple question, yet so... complex.* "Me? I'm simply a man with a given name. I have no identity anymore..." The woman turned around with a cup of water in her hand and gave a bewildered look in response. She seated herself by the frail, old man and pushed the cup of water towards him. "What's your name then?" He shot his eyes up at her, chuckled lightly, and responded, "My name?" The woman nodded in such a way that she seemed to emit some palpitating maternal energy. A type of trusting nod that made you feel secure. Like you could say anything to the woman in that moment. "Azubuike. That's my name. Call me Azu, please." He took a sip of his water and looked on, waiting for a response from the intrigued figure in front.

"Found you in a bad way, Azu. Found you outside passed out

on the streets. Thought I'd bring you in." Azu smiled and shook her arm with gratitude. "Thank you... I do appreciate it. It's been months since I've seen sunlight. I was trapped in a cell. The light and heat hit me and all of a sudden I was just so... overwhelmed. By all of it. And all of a sudden, I wake up in a bed and here you are. And you know the funniest thing. You, my child, are the closest I have to family. And I don't even know your damn name!" He didn't know whether to laugh or cry, and ended up doing neither, and finished his cup of water. "Lena... My name is Lena. You can stay here with me. I don't have much family either, except my son."

Azu circled his head quickly and looked around with weakened eyes at his new home. A small, compact little home with the light, barely audible snores of a sleeping child that could be heard from one of the rooms. "You mentioned a cell. How'd you get out? Or in?" Azu rubbed his eyes and replied brokenly, "A long story which I will find the time to tell you one day. But I was just let out. One day the doors opened, and they simply said 'out' and just like that... I'm a free man. But I've never realised freedom can taste so sour without family. There's nothing to it. I was walking straight and the light got so intense, and I could hear every voice in that market. I couldn't take it."

Lena held his hand and smiled at him, soothing him and calming him down. "Don't worry. Stay here. I'll take care of you. What's mine is yours Azu." Azu got up, walked a few steps and stared off into the wall, murmuring to himself. "That's interesting... I just had a thought Lena." Lena got up and stepped towards him cautiously, asking, "What is it?" Azu pivoted on his heels facing the confused woman and whispered, "I'm actually free..."

Then with some increased intensity, he said confidently, "I'm free Lena!" He leaned on the wall with his back, and slid down vertically against it to the floor, breaking down into a river of tears, and grasping his pounding head. Lena crouched down, seating herself next to him on the floor, holding his head to her shoulder and comforting the miserable, old man. *'Oh what am I going to do with you, old man'*, she thought to herself, stroking his head.

Chapter 1: Origins

"The course of love never did run smooth"-**A Midsummer Night's Dream** by *William Shakespeare*

Kanek Agrinya was sold at an auction, and bound in manacles to be shipped to America. He was broad-shouldered with a strong and Herculean build, with prominent deltoids. His voice was bold, and spoke as if his words held weight, reinforced by his orotund sense of speech. There were distinct scars on his upper left calf and bicep, the bloody marks of a cat o'nine whip. It was 20th April 1651, and Kanek was lying horizontally to other unfortunate slaves in the lower decks of the starboard of the vessel, locked in a chained embrace of manacles, unable to move.

"Life out o' dese manacles is real brothas, complete wid all tha luxuries we need." That was the perpetuating mantra groaned by Kanek, with minimal words that he could utter. He was in a stationary form of torture, and his neck was the only mobile area of his body, which he turned to face the person beside him, to which he responded, "How wud you live dat life brotha?" Kanek smirked upon hearing this question, accompanied with a flurry of hypothetical situations and his past, binding together inextricably, whilst looking off at the soft, yellow glow of the lantern that was suspended above him.

His vivid thoughts flashbacked to the summer of 1636, when he was youthful and full of energy working in the plantations in the Caribbean Isles, before the Atlantic trade system became more active. Kanek was working for a white entrepreneur called Cheval, who owned areas within the Caribbean archipelago, and funded money into the slave trade industry. His primary job was to hack sugarcanes in the plantation and load the stacks into crates to be shipped off to New England, using a machete.

Hours after midnight, a decade and a half later, Kanek was securing several sugarcanes, under the supervision of two guards and glimpsed upon a woman who had just left the house in the middle of the property. She had a unique skin complexion, in which her cheeks were rose and warm, in contrast with the bright highlights of white, spread along her skin. Her eyes were a sharp and vibrant blue, as if she had a ring of tropical sea sealed in her irises. She traversed delicately and her steps seemed almost calculated with every movement she took, as she made her way down the staircase at the entrance of the house.

Kanek was consumed by her beauty, and froze; his eyes trained specifically on her. They were locked in eye contact, and he could immediately view his life outside of the sorry reality he was living in, murmuring, "That's tha girl." A bright future within the fantasy in his mind. That was until the guard noticed his eyes wandering off, screaming, "The hell you think you're looking at you dirty scoundrel! Get back to work or I'll have Lord Cheval flog you himself for taking an interest in his daughter! A foreign wretch like you could not possibly stand a chance."

Kanek felt his blood boil in exasperation, as every bone in his body nudged him to lash out and crush the souls out of their bodies, ending their xenophobic rage, until she smiled. A smile so mesmerising that it cooled the fiery, livid passion within his body, which allowed him breathe calmly, and open his palms from tight fists. He felt the essence of love wash through his veins, subduing his wrath.

The sugarcanes were fastened and secured, then placed in the crates, ready for shipment, but his mind was fixated on that memory of her, and the passionate smile she presented alongside it; her teeth gleaming in the moonlight. It was as if every thought and image that had passed in his mind had her smile resonating within it, warming his heart. His lovestruck state caused him to feel the need to chase this fantasy, and although hope rendered him disadvantaged, in hand with reality, he was determined to obtain the impossible in the name of love. Kanek was not accustomed to the strength of love or even love itself, but viewed it as false and imaginary abstract concept that was just written or discussed about.

He viewed love to be existent only in the presence of family, and relatives, and that attraction felt towards women was not love but an extreme feeling of appeal. His mother would reinforce the concept of love to be real and true, and that it allows one to feel so satisfied, that there was no force that could ever exist to taint the feeling of pure love. So, with the goal set firmly in his mind, setting himself oblivious to the risks and unlikelihood of something existing between them, he walked along contentedly, with a smile stretched along his face, ready to enter the gates of Hell, to strike his reward. He did not even know of her name but he would not allow himself to be thrown off-course from his goal over the absence of that detail. So, he waited in vigil until the coming hours of daylight the next day, where he would begin his steps to being with her.

"Wake up, wake up, you filthy wretch! Lord Cheval needs have a word with you. Didn't sound so happy. Ha, gotta be good news if you're getting beat again, not like you have parents to run to afterwards, just your sorry excuses for friends!" Kanek stared at the guard, grinding his teeth and breathing heavily. He tightened his fists and got up, ready to confront Cheval, and hear what he had to say. They walked along the path, heading towards the main property in the estate, while the guards shovelled rum down their throats and continually insulted Kanek in their drunken mindset, taunting him continuously.

Just before Kanek was driven to his epitome of his anger, she walked by on the pathway, in the opposite direction to him, with the same, warm smile from when he last saw her. She seemed so in sync with nature, as if the morning birds were fluttering around her, and her steps made the grass and orchards greener. Her breath seemed to spread the essence of life through the acres of land around her, and the air felt so clean and fresh when he was in her presence. She stepped past, humming melodies and embracing nature, until one of the guards gripped her arm tightly and pulled her close. "Is there anything I could help you lovely gentlemen with? If you require refreshments, there is always access to tea and water in the house. Should I prepare some tea?"

The guards smirked, letting out moronic laughs, and murmuring crude comments to each other.
"Yea Daisy, the onl' thing you should prepare is yourself for us. Ol Cheval don' need to know does 'ee?" Kanek whispered to himself, "Daisy, so tha's yur name." Daisy, in a desperate attempt to stray from them shouted, "How disgusting of you men to treat me like dirt, when I have been nothing but respectful. Let go of me!" She tried to pull her arm back from them, but they continued to harass her, grabbing her waist, and ignoring her pleads to stop.

Kanek witnessed this, and was immediately filled with rage, as he closed his eyes and let the vexation flow through his body, and manifest inside of him. He harnessed this inner violent aura, and used it against the guards. He gripped onto one of the guard's shoulders, and faced towards him. He stared into his light yellow eyes and fired a punch to his jaw, then pinning him to the muddy, brown floor. The guard had blood in his mouth, as he gasped for breath, but Kanek's apoplectic rage did not calm, so he did not withdraw. The alarm bell was sounded and guards were closing in on Kanek's location, but at this point the guard was at the point of losing consciousness.
Until he came. Cheval Jean-Patrice. Ready to hunt his prey.

The air surrounding Kanek began to feel cold, and there was an unsettling silence, that scared him, causing him to freeze, and not land another punch. He could feel the anger emanating from the savage mob near him, as he prepared himself to face Cheval, with limited reason and explanation. Cheval had distinguishing features such as the scar on his left eye, partially blinding him. He had a sharp moustache, shaven beard and long hair, which unfolded upon his black and maroon robes. Kanek rose to his feet, with a bone-chilling shiver down his spine, and with shame explicitly viewed in his eyes.

Cheval gave off a cold smile, chuckling almost sadistically as he said, "So, you are Kanek. A strong fighter I must admit, but I was looking to lose a few guards anyway." Cheval aimed the gleaming musket in his arms at the downed guard and fired a round, killing him, as a stream of blood carried the life out of his body. Kanek was still, head held high, trying to eliminate any symptoms of intimidation. "I am a reasonable man Kanek, believe it or not. I ask my men to do a job, and they are expected to do that job, as that is why I've chosen them for. That demonstration you just witnessed was a man who couldn't do a job I asked him to, which was to bring you to me. So, it was clear there was no reason for him to keep doing that job. So, I liberated him. Would you like liberation, Kanek?"

Kanek did not respond, knowing what his *'liberation'* entails, as he viewed him reload his gun, ready to fire again. He saw Daisy within the crowd of bloodhounds for guards, with tears cascading down her cheeks, which struck a strong feeling of worry within him, as if they had shared the same predicament. "That death you just viewed was a result of your anger and choices. If you had allowed him to do his job rather than stop him taking you to me, then I would not have had to liberate him. He would still be alive. Breathing. With blood pumping through his veins if you had thought carefully. You caused this and I ended it." Kanek felt his stomach churn, consumed with guilt, regardless of his acknowledgement that he actually saved his daughter. But Cheval didn't know that.

He sweated heavily, knowing what he had just caused, barely able to look at Daisy. He was severely ridden with regret. Kanek asked with excessive fear and doubt, "What happun' now?" Cheval started to laugh callously, and simply replied, "I will not kill you. Nor will I kill your friends. But the liberation I offer you will set you on a bigger journey. Away from here, away from your friends. I will offer them no comfort in your absence, and you will leave knowing you will never see them again. Refuse this offer or you will suffer the fate of the moron beside your feet."

Kanek looked down at the lifeless guard by him in anger, but knew the decision he was making. So, he prepared himself for a long journey away from what he considered family.

Before he was set to leave the following day, he had gone to seek his friends to say goodbye. Kanek searched the whole compound to find them, but they were missing, which evoked anxiety within him. He decided to walk down the fresh streams cutting from the plantation to a nearby jungle, to clear his mind, until he heard noises in the distance suddenly break his peace. "*Arghhhhhhh!* Stop stop sto-*arghhh*!" Kanek followed the sound of raucous screams of pain, barging through vegetation and brambles, ignoring the scratches and cut skin on his body, with the determination of finding them. He eventually managed to track down the sound to a small camp within the jungle, outside the plantation, where he found his friends alive. But unapproachable. The camp was abundant with guards, armed with furnished rapiers and maces, scouting the area, so Kanek remained hidden in the bushes, waiting.

One of his friends was fastened to a rack, being tortured, whilst the others were kicked, stabbed and whipped until exhaustion. A tear rolled down his cheek, knowing that he could not save them, and that he had to leave the premises before he was to join them, although he had an unusual feeling of deja-vu. A guard, sitting by the fire, peered over the entrance of his tent and saw a silhouette of a figure lurking in the shadows, asking for who it is. With a heart filled with regret, he paced himself back to the plantation, not looking back, acknowledging that he would never see them again. He went back to his quarters; a cramped room with several other slaves wallowing in their own sweat, until he waited to disembark to the auction the next morning, alone with only anger and shame swimming around in his mind.

Chapter 2: Family Problems

"Tha's how I ended up in dis god-forsaken ship. No fam'ly. No idea of who I am. You're my fam'ly now..." exclaimed Kanek, as he managed to break out of his reminiscent mindset, and as if he were trapped in memories for comfort, and a burst of temporary happiness. A slave turned to him having listened to his past, with nothing but sorrow felt for Kanek's circumstances. "Brother, we live dis life to serve others because of who we are perc'ived as. We're objects, to ev'ryone we speak. Liberation does not com' to us. We live dis horrific curse, plagu'd upon us by society, 'cause of the 'impurity' dat spreads along our skin. Our colour is cherished in our culture, it is who we ar'. But it is poison. A flame that attracts society to bre'k us. But we'll not be brok'n."

Kanek listened intently with respect of his perception regarding race. But he did not consider his life to have any meaning if it did not uphold any element of grace and freedom. Being stripped of those concepts, rendered him more restrained than the manacles that held him, strapped to his bed. "Liberation's inevitable brother. We're human, we t'ink and feel tha same as others. We can ach'eve it," whispered Kanek, as he smiled and closed his eyes, preparing to rest. His throat was dry and parched, making it difficult for him to breathe. His joints were sore and painful, which delivered jabs of abrupt anguish in any attempt to move. He took a deep breath and laid still, trying desperately to fall asleep, until he is swept away by another memory, dragging him back to the moments of his childhood, that he had spent with his mother, after the early death of his father.

<u>*1622*</u>

"Kanek, com' fo' breakfast, we have t'go church. Eat ya food, 'nd we can go togetha." It was a balmy Sunday morning, with a pleasant wave of heat, submerging the streets of Imota, home to many in Lagos. Kanek flickered his eyes open, upon hearing his mother's distressed voice, and forced his body erect, to get ready for church. He made his way to the kitchen, having just washed himself quickly with the little remnants of water left in the well, to start on his breakfast. His mother scraped what was left of the rice from the sides of the container, and accompanied it with some vegetables, grown on her land. "I'm not hungry", Kanek stated monotonously upon viewing what was served, pushing the plate away from him.

His mother proceeded to pick the plate up, and clean it, whilst Kanek dressed himself, preparing for Sunday morning prayer. There was a noticeable sense of worry and concern in her face; her eyes slowly accumulated tears and became watery. She had acted like this ever since her husband's funeral. Kanek felt an abundance of worry, coinciding with anxiety, when observing her mother's countenance.

Her smile seemed to act as a mask to her worry, but the origin of it seemed blurred. Kanek felt himself taking heavier breaths, with an array of goose bumps scattered along his skin, with no understanding as to why. She wiped away her tears and whispered, "Let's leave fo' church now boy, rememba t'go outside afta we're done. I need to talk wid Pastor John about a few t'ings okay?" Kanek nodded, and proceeded to follow his mother out, to go to church. Something felt oddly wrong about going to church that Sunday, but he did not take heed of it.

The door creaked and groaned upon being opened by Kanek,

feeling almost like a warning to him. Something dark was consuming his thoughts, upon seeing how her mother was acting earlier, which caused him to freeze. The church was quiet, and Kanek was unable to move. "Wha's wrong darling?" whispered his mother soothingly. He looked up at her, and saw her smile, with shards of colour splashing upon her skin, from the stain-glass windows. It was as if the atmosphere of the church had washed away her anxiety and worry, which then had the same effect on him, giving him a feeling of liberation.

He found it easier to breath, and was calm; his emotions synchronised with his mother's. Without delay, they both headed to a pew to sit, and do their Sunday morning prayer. "Father, we are thankful for today. We pass this joyous day to the clasps of your heavenly hands. May we be at ease in your spiritual presence, consumed in your benevolence, and admire your eternal life. Amen."

The congregation stated "Amen" in perfect harmony, in reply to John, who his mother shared an unusual liking to. She had often praised him to relatives, making him to be a hero, and how his words spread joy with every syllable, and how his faith in Christianity was admirable. Kanek could not recognise why her mother was upset but had figured out what had led to her sudden change of emotion. "I knew it! That man's no hero", Kanek whispered as he closed his eyes, and calmed his anger.

The morning prayers had soon come to an end and a few of the congregation prepared to leave. Kanek grabbed his mother's wrist with a tight grip, repeatedly saying "Le's go, I'm hungry", dragging her towards the doors. Kanek's mother gave him a stern look, and responded, "Lemme talk to Pastor John about som' of my worries. Go play football wid ya friends, I'll make yu food when we get hom'. Just don' turn it down dis time."

Kanek searched every crevice of his mind for a possible reason as to why he should listen to his mother, but ended up realising that he had no power over her choices, so he left, waiting by the patches of grass outside of the church.

"Com' on Kanek, play football wid us and stop bein' so moody!", moaned all his friends, as Kanek laid still against a tree, with a gaunt, solemn expression spread out along his face. Kanek turned his head towards them, and observed their cheerful smiles. He then slowly helped himself up onto his feet, and felt more determined to not allow his dark thoughts to consume him, by adding joy. He walked towards the ball, with a smile on his face, and shouted, "Com' on, le's play somet'ing", which presented an obvious excitement on his friend's face. Just as the game was about to kick off, there was an abrupt sound of breaking glass, as well as, screams and cries that accompanied the harmony of chaos, shooting out of the church, which caused Kanek to run frantically towards the church, consumed by more than just curiosity.

"Run, run away from 'ere! They hav com'. Dreadful vermin!,"screamed an individual from within the church. Kanek peered from the side of the entrance, crouching upon pieces of broken oak, to view the hectic interior of the church. White men armed with muskets and wheellocks, were grappling onto people, and knocking them unconscious, to escort them out of the area, with less resistance. When Kanek looked back, he found his friends captured and moved towards a wooden cart for extraction, which led to him feeling extremely irate, but knew his only hope to save himself was to enter the church, as guards had locked down the church's exits within a certain radius.

Kanek entered, and hid by the side of a pew, controlling his breathing, as his heart raced uncontrollably. "Let go! Let go please! I hav' a child, I can't leave h-" The guard struck the individual before she could finish her sentence, with no guilt expressed towards her pain, and pushed her onto the floor. "Move", the guard stated remorselessly, enforced with controlled anger. Kanek gazed at them, seeing his mother and the pastor, with little clothing, being dragged out of the church viciously.

His thoughts were right, concerning the pastor and his mother, and their illicit affair, but he stayed hidden, crying silently, knowing that he had witnessed his final glimpse of his mother. "That must be all of them, let's leave now. Have them rounded up at the rendezvous point!" shouted the main guard, as they left the premises. Kanek laid his head against the side of the pew, with a perpetuating river of tears that fell down his cheeks. His heart stopped racing, but he had reached a point where nothing could sustain happiness within him, and reverted to his gaunt, solemn countenance.

Chapter 3: The Battle

"It is for freedom that Christ set us free. Stand firm therefore, and do not submit again to a yoke of slavery"-**Galatians 5:1**

"*Arghh!*" Kanek woke up breathing fast, feeling scared and intimidated. His skin felt irritated from the masses of sweat splashing around, being unable to wipe it off, and had the feeling to itch in every point in his body. A guard waltzed in with a lantern to check on the noise, armed with a wheellock pistol and a sword. He stared at each slave, delivering an eerie look towards each poor soul, and even spat at a few.

"Eurgh, stinks in here," murmured the guard as he walked past slowly, observing the way they lied and breathed, which struck fear within them. Kanek tried to wriggle and pull himself out the manacles hopelessly, as the guard got closer; his head feeling lighter and hotter in return. The guard continued to walk forward, as if he were going to move past Kanek's bed, but halted. He let out a cold, quiet laugh, and turned his head to Kanek; his eyes bloodshot red.

He proceeded to move over him, his head close to Kanek's and whispered, "Scream like that again, and I'll cut your fingers and feed them to you. You mean nothing. You're nothing. You're nothing but a slave. You have no purpose, no honour, and certainly no freedom!" Kanek spat in his face with a serious look in his eyes. The guard moved a dagger in his pocket towards Kanek's neck, whilst the smell of rum from his breath started to overwhelm him.

The guard continued to say, "You think you're brave? Do you? I could finish your life right now; one death won't mean anything. But there's something different about you. In the way you act and look. What is it that you truly seek scum?" Kanek simply replied, "Freedom." The guard burst into uncontrollable laughter, and lifted the dagger above his head, ready to bring it down into his skull, and rid of him of his life. "Here's your freedom. Hope you enjoy it, you damn dog!", said the guard angrily.

"We're under attack! Man the cannons, and hold off the enemy ship!" screamed the captain on the top deck, from the top of his lungs. The guard froze confused, hearing cannon shots, and breaking wood and debris. "Incoming! Brace for impact!" A flurry of cannons penetrated the side of the frigate, and obliterated the sides of the slaver, breaking it down, and exposing the interior.

Kanek saw the valiant ocean for the first time in ages, the cold air soothing him. Kanek also saw the galleon that was attacking the frigate that he was on, through the non-existent walls, in front of him. A monster of ship, armed with uncountable cannons, and no damage dealt to it at all. "Oh, dear god" murmured Kanek in seeing the ship and began to panic, whilst every slave was perplexed and scared. "They're firing again damn it! Brace!" The entire ship was on high alert, and nearly no damage was dealt on the enemy ship.

The galleon had gotten closer to the frigate and fired its next set of rounds. Kanek saw the masses of smoke from its cannon as the cannonballs came shooting out of it and bombarded the ship. All that could be heard was the deadly loud shots of the cannon, and the coughing of the people on board from the dust and smoke submerging the ship. Then two cannons travelled majestically through the air towards the frigate, and as Kanek witnessed them, time slowed down.

It was as if everything had stopped and he could see each molecule of dust that moved past his eyes. The guard turned and looked at them, and realised for the split second that he was in danger, and he sighed, defeated. The cannon entered the ship and struck the floor near the guard, and ultimately bringing him down, as he slid across the floor and into the wall. The second cannon hit close to Kanek's manacles, shattering the chain, breaking it and freeing his left hand. The guard spat blood on the floor and struggled to breathe properly. He looked at Kanek and reached for his pocket and took out his keys and passed it to him stuttering, "Ea-rn yo-ur free-dom…"

Kanek grabbed the keys and frantically searched for the right ones to unlock his manacles. Amidst the chaos, Kanek successfully managed to free his fettered ankles from the manacles, whilst having a flurry of thoughts rushing through his head, feeling more excited with every lock that was opened. The third round of cannons were fired at the frigate, and shook the whole frame of the ship, causing Kanek to fall to the right on his side. After the final lock was released, Kanek's body was mobile, but he fell to the ground.

He had been locked up for so long that it felt impossible to move properly, but after having looked at his fellow brothers who needed his help, he found the power within himself to rise and help them. He worked his way towards one individual and freed him, holding him up and kept him stable. Kanek looked at him sternly and gave him commands, shouting, "Free ev'ry person on dis ship brotha and round dem up in tha ship's kitchen, since all tha guards must be busy defending tha ship so it'll be empty. I'm gonna try and secure dis ship." The man confusingly replied, "By you'self brotha!?" as to why anyone would suggest something that suicidal. Kanek calmly said, "Aye, it is the only way, if we ar' to live tha lifestyle we long for."

The slave nodded obediently, as Kanek ran towards the bleeding, unconscious guard, and grabbed his weapons. Kanek staggered along the pathway to the stairs that lead to the middle deck, placing the pistol and dagger between the wrapped red ribbon around his waist holding up his torn, cotton shorts, whilst having the sword in his hand. Upon reaching there, he found the armoury, which was now empty, giving off a desolate aura.

"Here we go, slave!," said the captain. Kanek turned around and heard another round of shots fired at the ship, and asked the captain, whilst they pointed their swords at each other, "Yur ship's unda' fire, yur men dying an' I'm the priority? Have yu no shame?" The captain replied, "You want to talk to me about shame boy? You disgusting creature! My men can hold their own, unlike you!" The captain lunged for a strike but Kanek parried the attack and swiped his thigh with the sword, then proceeds to hit his nose with the handle, to taunt him.

"You think you're smart? Do you!? I've been doing this all my life kid!" The captain struck again and Kanek managed to block the attack a second time, but they pushed the swords into each other, until Kanek barged him into wall causing him to drop his sword. He kicked his sword away and held the sword to his neck, ready to kill.

"Do it you coward! Show me your true colours! Spill my blood upon this ship and you'll see yourself who is the real villain here. You've never killed, have you?" Kanek felt his body get consumed by more and more rage; his arm started to shiver. "What's the problem? Your mum not here to hold your hand!?" the captain sneered, mocking him. Kanek no longer shivered, and maintained a strong posture aided by cold rage and said, "Yu t'ink I'm scared? Yu t'ink me so soft to not kill yu? My brothers yu hold in dis ship need freedom. They com' first. Not yu." Kanek, without hesitation killed the captain; his blood spilled across the wall. Kanek felt nauseated, with an urge to vomit on the floor, with his bloodstained hands and sword, feeling different and as if he were reborn.

As Kanek was about to leave, a guard caught him by surprise and struck his lower obliques, causing him to bleed profusely, and got kicked onto the floor. "Good job with killing the captain, you dog! Now you can go to hell and torment him!" Kanek reached for the wheellock pistol and fired a round at his chest, before he could strike. The guard dropped to his knees, feeling extreme anguish, and put his hand on his chest breathing heavily, and laughed lightly, uttering, "Lucky shot…" The guard proceeded to fall to the ground dead, and Kanek had developed a new sense of bloodlust. All in the name of freedom.

Seawater began to seep through the crevices in the floorboards, submerging Kanek's feet and dampening the sawdust into a cold, watery paste. The dead guards soon began to float and the blood from their lifeless bodies began to slowly draw out of the wounds, creating a puddle of raw gore for Kanek to trudge through, towards the stairs leading to the trapdoor. Kanek held desperately onto his wound trying to reduce the bleeding as he climbed slowly towards the ladder to leading to the trapdoor.

"That bastard! I feel so weak an' feel as tho I ca'not continu' dis journ'y," cried Kanek, with tear-filled eyes and fell to his knees in utmost pain. The searing pain from the slit in his side was unbearable, and the gradual loss of blood drained the energy out of him. The fourth set of cannons pummelled the side of the ship, causing Kanek to stumble forward towards the ladder, clasping onto the lower rungs. Kanek looked up towards trapdoor, feeling a subtle breeze crawl along his skin. The feeling of the cold wind almost numbed the pain he was experiencing, and granted him a sudden burst of strength to climb the ladder.

The blood began to run in lines down his obliques and stained his pants, making maroon ovals along the lining. Kanek's grip became increasingly stronger as he forced himself up the ladder, as he felt his muscles tighten and his breaths getting more controlled. There was a euphoric feeling, the higher Kanek had made it up his ladder, every bit higher he had gotten, made him feel liberated. Until he had reached the trapdoor.

Kanek felt a gateway to new life just beyond it. He knew that he had one shot to save everyone he cared for, by fighting his way through the bloodbath he was about to enter. After having acknowledged the dangerous mission he was about to undergo, he opened the trapdoor.

Chapter 4: A Warrior is Born

As soon as Kanek nudged the trapdoor, the wind flung it open, smashing onto the surface. A robust storm brewed whilst the ship was taking damage, with lightning, rain and wind overwhelming the vulnerable ship. As he popped his head out, a mixture of rain and blood had swept the deck of the ship, as the gigantic Poseidon of a storm slowly crushed the ship into the depths of Davy Jones' Locker. The foamy sea began to spray the crew of the ship, as the vessel rattled and the wood shattered everywhere. Kanek dragged his body towards two barrels and rested his back on it, as he applied pressure on his wound.

The blood seemed to seep through his fingers and stray away with the heavy rain, until he found a wet piece of long cloth lying stuck under one of the barrels. Resting his bloodied hand on the floor, Kanek desperately tried to pull the cloth out, resulting in the barrel toppling over. The chaotic crew diverted their attention to him, calling viciously to the remainder of their men, to tear the life out of his weakened body. Wrapping the cloth haphazardly around his body, and sealing the wound, Kanek witnessed the frigate's wheel at the other end of the sinking ship. This sparked a near suicidal idea in his mind, and forced himself up in order to initiate it. The raging waves of the sea began to climb higher, as the fifth set of cannon fire decimated the crew, leaving fewer to defend.

As Kanek strafed the ship, heading towards the wheel, he butchered the remainder of the crew who lay in his path, slicing a gory path to his goal. Minutes flew by and the pain in his obliques began to intensify, which caused him to clench tighter to his sword, as he took a gun from one of the dead guards. In a matter of minutes, Kanek found himself at the captain's wheel, ready to begin his perilous plan.

Kanek stared at the galleon, gripping hard onto the wheel, ready to begin. Without hesitation, he span the wheel rapidly, and rammed the dilapidated remains of the frigate onto the port side of the monster of a vessel. The sixth set of cannons tore into the interior of the boat in response, leaving the vessel to sink, as the incensed waters began to slowly consume the debris. The mast of the frigate began to plummet, as the sails detached and fell onto the majority of the rubble.

Then he remembered. His brothers who were holed up in the ship's kitchen. This led him into the second stage of his plan, the deadly stage. The only hope of victory. Commandeering the galleon, and allowing his fellow people to board. Despite the unlikeliness of surviving, he knew it was the only way. After having spent little time to acknowledge what he was about to do, he leapt onto the side of the galleon and scaled the side of it. As he climbed aboard, he saw countless, merciless crew, who began to draw their swords and look at him menacingly, and Kanek unsheathed his sword in return, ready to engage with the bloodthirsty dogs.

A myriad of metallic clangs began to spread like a swarm of deadly locusts along the air, as the obstreperous, savage group attacked him. "He's killing our crew you worthless men! I want him captured now!" screamed the captain of the ship. Amongst the chaos, Kanek managed to shift his focus to him for a second; time seemed to halt as his vision was solely focused on the captain. He wore a long black robe, with white lining, along with tough, leather boots, brown beard and deep blue eyes. There was an evident ominousness reflected in his very being; a sad, almost threatening look seemed to emerge from his face. That second of observation was enough distraction for the crew to overcome Kanek's might, and soon enough he found himself staring at the point of a sword, lying on the ground as the crew began to pick him up and make him kneel before him. The captain.

"Welcome aboard! Glad you had fun slicing up my crew but everyone needs a break from doing what they love, it's just not healthy to not have breaks, isn't it? Name's Garrett by the way!", said Garrett, walking slowly in circles around him, unsheathing his jaded sword. Kanek looked up at him, seeming almost fearless in his expressions. "I didn' enjoy killin' ya men; I had no choice. It was-" Kanek was cut off by his distasteful laughter.

"You didn't enjoy it? What a liar! You enjoyed every second of it, you maniac! I could see it in your eyes. The way you stared into their eyes when you shoved your sword into their insides. I know that feeling. That fizzy, but potent feeling within you when you spill blood. We're both as psychotic as each other. And I'm going to leave you falling down this maddening abyss with me. Bring him to side. I want him to see this." The crew dragged Kanek towards the side of the stern of the ship to gaze upon the slave ship in front of him.

"Man the cannons, one more round should send that ship down under, and that's just it boy, you'll never see your friends again. They will be nothing but corpses just floating around in a wreck underwater. Fish food essentially. I mean I initially just needed the resources from their ship. They refused. So here we are." At this point, Kanek began to panic, realising fully what Garrett was going to. What he considered family, blown to shreds with iron cannons, and buried in the murky depths of the ocean. "I won' let yu! Yu damn'd bastard!" screamed Kanek, as the crew began to grip him tighter and away from the side. The seventh round of cannons. The final round of cannons. There was a loud bang, and the slaver began to crumble and sink, as the galleon began to set sail away from the wreck.

"Your mind is mine now" whispered Garrett in his ear. A sudden rush of fiery anger began to consume Kanek, his muscles tightened and breaths deeper and more frequent. In an instant, he tore his arm from the guard's grip, and struck Garrett's face, stunning him. He then proceeded to latch onto his jaded sword, and jumped off the ship, into the stormy, cold waters, hoping to survive somehow. "Oh my god, argh, tha waters ar' too strong", spluttered Kanek, gasping for air, whilst constantly spitting out the saltwater that seeped into his mouth.

He saw the slaver slowly begin to submerge, causing him to frantically swim towards the wreckage, to attempt to save his friends. "Here goes not'ing!" he shouted before diving underwater. The salt from the water began to sting Kanek's eyes, as he forced himself deeper and deeper into the water, until he found the entrance to the wreck via a blown out hole in the side of frigate. Pressure began to slowly lock and crush his skull, as he started to lose more and more air.

Until he could see a woman floating in the water, with her hair unfolded and spread along the water. He swam towards the unconscious body, as the wreck continued to descend and light was getting less prominent. He untied the red, long ribbon along his waist and tied her wrists together, and sheathed the sword and dagger on the strong harness that kept her clothes on. He proceeded to place her on his back and used the tied arms as his way of dragging her to the surface without having to hold her.

Kanek began to swim frantically towards the surface, nearly out of breath. He felt his body undergo a painful, crushing feeling. His lungs were near empty and felt his rib-cage cave in, as every part of his body was severely deprived of the touch of air. Until he made it. "Oh God, oh god, I could only save one woman. I did dis. They finish' tha ship off cuz o' me. All ova sum stupid raid fo' supplies", shouted Kanek, blinking forcefully, trying to regain his peripheral vision. Once his vision returned, he was able to see a small, white whaleboat floating near him with a few people within it, shouting at him to get into it. He moved close to the boat and they dragged him into it but passed out before he could say anything. His vision faded into darkness.

"Look who's decided to join us!" Kanek woke up to see the blurred figures of three men and the woman he saved, but as his eyesight began to focus; one man stood out from all the men. A white figure, with red streaks along his face. As his eyes adjusted and his vision returned, he realised who he was looking at. It was the unconscious body of the guard who had attempted to plunge a dagger into his skull. "Now dere's a face I t'ought I'd neva see. Tha bastard surviv'd? As much as I want t'plunge my sword into his chest and let'im bleed out in tha ocean, we owe our freedom to him. I won' kill him for dat reason alone," said Kanek, smiling at his new friends amongst the little whaleboat.

One man stepped up and grabbed the oars and began moving the boat, while the others began to rest, replying "We weren't planning on it either boy..." The man looked up at Kanek, and stared, dragging the heavy boat with ease. The others began to drift into sleep, as the storm had come to a quiet finish. There was a golden landscape, as the light began to interweave and mix with the soft clouds, and the sea was still, with only the mild ripples of the oars cutting through. "Wat is yur name? An' where are tha others?", asked Kanek inquisitively, with a hint of worry.

The man lifted his eyes, and gave him another long stare. He wore rags, and had a black, tangled beard. His eyes were yellow with blood clots, and had heavy breaths. He looked old but somewhat wise and strong, with veins laid like roots along his arms, and opened his mouth to speak. "My name is Azubuike, but everyone calls me Azu, and your friends had to leave boy. But we couldn't. Even in the chaos and gunfire, we had to stay.."

Kanek, confused, proceeded to ask, "Why?", with profound respect for his ability to speak with a somewhat good English accent. Azu looked to the woman lying at the edge of the boat, with a warm smile.

"She's a pearl, is she not? Her name's Dara, and we don't know what we would do without her. I found her deserted near a well crying as a child, and I raised her as my own. Everything was great, up until my house was raided and we were both captured. And I swore I would treat her like my daughter; she deserved better than abandonment and abuse.

Loyalty runs deep in our deep in our blood boy, as for us to be able to flourish and work, we must act as a family, not a team, you understand?" Azu stated sternly at Kanek, to which he replied with a nod. "My name is Kanek by tha way. Thanks fo' savin' us, I'll stand by all of yu." Azu simply replied, "You are family now, even this 'bastard' lying beside us. We'd all be dead without each other. Get some rest." Crawled up the corner of the whaleboat, Kanek began to slowly shut his eyes, readying himself for what the future would hold.

Chapter 5: Marooned

"Would you tell me, please, which way I ought to go from here?'
'That depends a good deal on where you want to get to,' said the Cat.
'I don't much care where -' said Alice.
'Then it doesn't matter which way you go,' said the Cat.
'- so long as I get SOMEWHERE,' Alice added as an explanation.
'Oh, you're sure to do that,' said the Cat, 'if
you only walk long enough.'

-Alice in Wonderland by *Lewis Carroll*

Blood. Pain. Torture. Kanek found himself bound by cold, iron manacles digging into his wrists, as faceless entities zoomed past. Terrifying whispers, and an essence of death began to fill the dark room, and his struggling only made the pain more intense. Blood began to draw out of cuts on his wrists and his breathing got more intense. Until one entity stopped, and reached its arm. Everything seemed monochrome and sadistic, as Kanek stared into the eyes of the beast as it approached closer. The creature became more and more vulgar, taunting him, scaring him, indulging in the fear that emanated from him.

The creature began to laugh and let out his tongue, ready to feast on the bones of his body. There was an evident lack of humanity, and Kanek's pleas for help had no effect. "Stay away, don' touch me! I won' let yu! I won' allow yu to dis to me! I'm not scared..." The creature grinned and laughed, gripping tightly onto his head, which stifled his voice.

Every breath it took began to overwhelm Kanek, and the grip got tighter and tighter. The jaws unhinged and it got ready to feed on its prey. And it struck! Kanek could do nothing but scream in terror. "*Arghh*, get off me get off ple-" Then reality hit. And he opened his eyes to find himself free of the nightmare, as the cold, tropical morning breeze, calmed his worry to nothing, as he lay shivering in the boat, speechless.

"Hold still, let me wrap that wound properly, the cloth is falling off." Kanek looked up to see Dara, smiling warmly at him. He smiled back, as he laid still, allowing her to treat the wound. As he peered over her shoulder, he noticed that they had arrived at a small speck of a sand island in the middle of the ocean. There was one palm tree and a massive rock, and the men were sitting around a fire, as they cooked fish on wooden sticks, and cracked open coconuts for water. "Thank you for saving me, they told me all about your amazing rescue, and how you dragged me out of the shipwreck and stormy sea. I can't thank you enough, Kanek, right?"

Kanek chuckled and replied, "Yea, yu are right, can't miss that amazin' long hair anywhere." Dara rubbed Kanek's cheek, letting out a little laugh and helped him up and out of the boat, to join the others. "My name is My name is Dara by the way." He looked to the left as he walked, and saw the saved guard holding a small bottle in his hand, sitting down and drunk, whilst he rested his head on the rock, isolated from the group. "Yu go on ahe'd Dara, I'll join yu people later, I won' be long." Dara gave a prompt hug and went to join the others.

"Ay, yu bastard, guess yu can say I've earn' my freedom now right? I prefer being on a tiny island to hav'ng the freedom yu were suggesting. Ironic how yu have to get along wid me afta callin' me 'nothing but a filthy slave'" said Kanek, crouching in front of him, smirking. The guard pushed his head up, laughing and saying, "They should have left me on that godforsaken ship.

Better than sharing an island with you freaks. And that woman I saw you with, on the boat, you sure she ain't some whore that gets passed around. I mean don't worry, if I had her I wouldn't. Would want all of that to myself. The name's Gunner by the way, not bastard. But I think 'bastard' suits you, though I don't know if whore and bastard go well together tho."

A roar of drunken laughter escaped his mouth, as he pointed and jeered at him. Kanek snatched the stoneware bottle and took a sip, and slammed it into the sand, as the contents leaked out. He then proceeded to grab his throat and took out a dagger, and placed it near his eyes, with a stern look on his face.

"You rememba dis Gunner, rememba dis blade, well if yu ever talk about her or any of tha othas like dat, I promise yu, I will be tha one granting you freedom, not yu. I will chuck ya corpse into tha ocean. Don' even try to kill me. 'Cause one way or anotha you'll wound up dead. Dis is my family. Name's Kanek by tha way." Kanek flipped the dagger and placed it back under his ribbon, and let go of his neck, as Gunner gasped for breath, with an annoyed but somewhat worried look on his face.

"Come and join us Kanek. We saved some coconut water and fish for you. Catfish. You can tell by the 'whiskers' sticking out. It's definitely a good catch. You saved Dara, and in return, we must give you the best of whatever we have," exclaimed Azu, laughing happily. He moved toward Kanek, and proudly grabbed his arm and lifted it into the air, shouting, "Kanek, our saviour, and now family!" They began to cheer, and there was a strong sense of elation shared between the group. They brought the catfish and coconut water to him, as they sat around the fire, and rested. Azu sat closer to Kanek, and spoke quietly, familiarising him with everyone.

"Well, we have Ebenezer, and you've already met Dara. Ebenezer is the brute, the person you go for when in need of backup, or just strength. I've seen him lift more than two of us put together.

I don't know the guards name though. I trust you will find out," said Azu. "Gunner, his name's Gunner", said Kanek, as he proceeded to eat the remaining chunk of fish, and threw the skeleton away. He began to rest his eyes, as he lay comfortably on the soft, cold sand, staring mindlessly into the clouds, as a smile began to appear along his face, knowing he was in good hands, and with thoughts of Dara running through his mind. Once again, his mind began to explore more hypothetical situations, as he began to indulge in a strong love that took over his thought and soul.

There was a zephyr that began to travel along the sea to the island, as it lulled the group to sleep, and a vale of darkness spread along the sky, and the stars began to disperse. Kanek sat awake, examining the dagger. There was a strange sigil that was engraved on it, of a red, tangled dragon, spread vertically on the blade along with the message, *'Fear the Order, Submit to the Bloody Three, or the Red Amphiptere will find and murder thee'*. But he paid it no mind. He walked into the waters to bathe, as the cold, calm waters freshened his senses, and provided a sense of strong comfort. "Ah, tha waters ar' so much better wen they're not tryin' t'devour yu. Still quite cold tho. But betta' than bathing in sweat.

But Kanek spotted something off into the distance, almost hidden in the night sky. Two spots of yellow gleaming off into the distance. A ship? Kanek could not make out what it was. But it was stationary, and had an unorthodox livelihood seeping off it, so he quickly decided to investigate the mysterious light. He ran to the whaleboat and armed himself with the sword, and pushed it out onto the water. Having taken the oars, he began to row the boat out into the open sea. The boat started to rattle lightly, as the winds began to get colder and rowdy.

Thud! Something had hit the base of the boat, and the whole boat began to rattle more vigorously. Kanek rowed more quickly, with anxiety, mixed with perplexity. "Wat is lurking beneath me?" he asked himself. The boat was rattling uncontrollably at this point, causing Kanek to grip tightly onto the side. The crates began to shimmy out and he found it harder and harder to remain still, until it happened. A humpback whale propelled out of the water, spearing majestically into the air.

Time began to slow down again as he saw it. He felt every drop of water hit his head, as it flew past, until reality hit again, and the whale came crashing down back into the water. The shockwave lifted the front of the boat higher into the air, as Kanek tumbled onto the other side, and the gelid waters began to fill the interior. "Now dat's not somet'ing yu see ev'ryday? Such a beautiful creature!" Kanek proceeded to laugh quietly to himself in awe and amazement.
The waters returned to its tranquility, and he proceeded to row again. A silhouette of the vessel began to appear. A seemingly small frigate was in front was visible in front.

There were overwhelming alcoholic fumes that came off the ship, accompanied by loud shrieks and laughter. Kanek looked up to see an open window in the ship's stern, and brought his whaleboat closer towards it. He climbed the rear of the ship, abandoning the whaleboat and climbing onto the vessel, and went in through the window. The smell of liquor and rum got more overpowering, and the irrepressible laughter of the crew became more deafening. A man stood weak and exhausted, with his hands suspended to the ceiling, covered in cuts and bruises.

Two drunken armed men came tumbling into the room laughing, one holding a bottle, and Kanek crouched behind a pillar and remained still, and had his hand by his sword ready. "Ay there, Cain, you doin' good down 'ere? Needa lil drink?" bellowed the first guard, and started to pour rum over his face, as he gasped for breath. "Huh, not gonna say anythin'? 'Ave it your way, I'm still gonna 'ave fun punchin' your ribs in…" The guard began to punch the man to the chest and head mercilessly, as he tried to repress his pain. The second guard tumbled towards the window, drunk and nauseous. Kanek stayed absolutely quiet, as he stumbled past. The other guard stopped hitting Cain, and proceeded to look at something on the table, facing away from them.

Dagger in hand, Kanek sneaked towards the guard at the window, clasped his hand onto his mouth, stabbed him with it, deep into the chest, until he felt no breaths on his palm, and then retracted his hand, and pushed him out of the window.

The raucousness of the crew shielded the sound of his fall into the water, and he looked to the next guard. With worries running through his mind, he sneaked quietly towards the guard with the bloody dagger, the floorboards began to let out loud creaks and noises. His pace got slower and slower, the closer he got to the guard, with his heart beating thunderously. "The Order of the Red Amphiptere? You're one of them?" bellowed Cain, staring at Kanek. "Oh shutup, you lousy piec-" The guard had a moment of shock, before he reached for his sword, to which Kanek retaliated by stabbing him repeatedly until he stopped struggling, silencing him.

Grabbing a chair, Kanek barricaded the door leading into the room, and helped Cain by cutting the rope holding him. "Yu could hav' said that nonsense afta I dealt wid tha idiot in front of me. What were yu on 'bout? Red Amphi- wat?"

There was a sense of confusion in Cain's eyes, and replied saying, "It's a type of dragon. Winged serpents." Kanek looked with confusion and worry. "You know wha- your sword. It's a rare jaded sword, with the Amphi-dragon, my bad, sigil. No one is to own one except elite members of the Order. It belongs to-" Kanek interrupted, with his cutting rejoinder, "Garrett?"

Cain let out an unorthodox laugh, and responded by saying, "So you know him? He's one of the three main men that uphold the order. Garrett, Cheval and Haines. The Order was set up a decade ago, and the purpose of the group is to ensure that they can acquire enough resources and money to be able to buy themselves massive control over the Atlantic slave trade, so that they can conduct their own plans." Kanek sat on the floor and listened.

"Cheval? Cheval Jean-Patrice? I kno' him. He was tha owner of a plantation I was pr'viously based at. He's psycho. Shot a guard out in front of me wid a musket, and tortur'd my fr'ends. Garrett isn' differ'nt eitha. Managed to take dis sweet blade off him, so it wasn' a complete loss. How were yu so sure it's his? I kno' it's jaded but it's still a sword, could belong to anyon'", whispered Kanek, with the sword in hand. Cain ran his fingers along the sword to the handle, and placed his finger on the bottom, and Kanek sees the same sigil on the dagger. A tangled red dragon. "I recognise dis. It's on dis dagga. Look it's tha same symbol. Red drag'n. Gunner, do yu kno' a Gunner?"

Cain placed his hand on Kanek's shoulders, and shook his head, and proceeded to say, "Calm down, it's an Order, meaning they have loads of followers. I won't know every individual. My main aim is to bring the big dogs down. They are responsible for me being here, tortured everyday. They sent men to ransack my manor, and stole everything. They kidnapped me, and hid me away on this ship for weeks. Guess it was their way of keeping me quiet."

Kanek let out a mild chuckle, helping Cain up, saying, "They're not very good at tyin' up loose ends, if I'm here rescuin' yu. Com' le's get yu out of here. Name's Kanek." Cain stopped Kanek, before he headed towards the window. "What are you doing? These men are drunk and vulnerable, and in no position to fight. We can easily commandeer this vessel", stated Cain enthusiastically and fearlessly.

There was a very clear reluctancy in Kanek's facial expressions, blended with confusion and slight worry, which resulted in him replying, "I don' kno' Cain, seems a bit risky for my liking. I hav' a whaleboat, I t'ink that should do tha job." Cain stared hardly at Kanek and laughed, and tapped his arm saying, "Oh Kanek, where's your sense of adventure and violence!? You got the warrior spirit in you. You certainly did tearing that guard apart! I have a plan, follow my lead and we can make it with a proper boat, you ready?" Kanek took a deep breath and replied sternly "Aye."

Chapter 6: A Thirst for Power

"Here they are, nice and light but destructive." Cain pulled out a crate from under the table, filled with ceramic hand grenades, resembling big pomegranates, and Kanek oblivious to what they are. "These are one of a kind Kanek, devastating power. Won't find these everywhere. Now, here's the plan. You climb back out of the window and onto the stern of the ship and wait for my signal before taking down the captain by the wheel. Do not kill him."

Kanek observed Cain's excited face, bewildered himself, and asked, "And what abou' tha otha membas of tha crew? I he'rd at least 10. And wat signal?" Cain gave off a confident smile, and answered, "You'll definitely know when you hear it, now get up there!" Kanek nodded obligingly, and paced back to window. He gripped firmly onto the ledges above him, to ensure he did not fall down, into the freezing waters. Kanek found himself in a very precarious position, the ledges getting thinner and thinner, which caused him to grip harder.

    He proceeded to grab the lantern fixed on the back of the ship, to help him reach the last ledge. But realised he made a mistake. The lantern began to break off, and Kanek about to follow with it, until he reached with his right arm, and managed to secure a grip on the final ledge, as the lantern plummeted into the water. He remained very still before climbing over and onto to stern, so that the captain does not spot him, and potentially ruin Cain's 'plan'.

After waiting, he climbed over and hid behind a barrel, waiting patiently to strike. The captain stood still by wheel, as he observed over his men, as they danced, drank, and sang sea shanties melodiously. The anticipation began to make Kanek sweat uncontrollably, as he waited for the signal, worried that he missed it, and thinking of everything that could jeopardise the plan.

Bang! Bang! Bang! There was a load of massive, ear-splitting sounds, and this prompted Kanek to run instinctively, as he pulled out his gleaming sword, and held it at the captain's neck, rendering him harmless. "Drop yur weapons and get on yur knees befo' I do somet'ing very distasteful," asserted Kanek, as he placed the sword, closer to his neck, grazing his skin. The captain obligated, and Kanek knocked him unconscious with the handle of the sword.

As Kanek walked towards the base of the central mast, he saw a floor covered with injured men, two dead, along with broken, shattered wood. There was puddles of blood, peppered with splinters of wood, pouring out everywhere, with splatters on the barrels and railings. What confused Kanek more than how this happened, was that he did not feel sick or bad about it. The blood did not faze him, and the guilt seemed non-existent. Walking past the corpses was like walking through a meadow, filled with aromatic flowers.

His lack of care for the dead and injured men on the floor, made him feel worse than if he had felt bad killing them. *'Is this who I am now? Merciless and unloving? I don't feel an ounce of compassion towards these men. Their pain-filled groans are nothing. I seek liberation. But I fear I will lose myself'*, thought Kanek to himself, as he looked around him at everyone. Kanek turned around to see Cain finishing off the injured men, killing them. But again he felt nothing. No drive or incentive to tell him that what he was doing was wrong. Kanek simply watched, as they all got killed by the point of Cain's blade. There was a clear rage within him, something wild.

"Well, that should be all of them. If you don't mind me asking, why did you get on this ship? What was the point? You must have known you would be outnumbered", asked Cain, as he lifted a bloodied corpse, throwing it overboard. Kanek remained silent.

There was something odd about Cain. He had slit eyebrows, and a patchy stubble, and his smile was eerie, not warm at all. Every piece of Kanek's mind was urging him to not trust him, to ignore him, and to leave the vessel, and that he was better off with the whaleboat. But practically, he did manage to secure a ship for them both, and it would be a jovial, convenient surprise for Dara, Azu, Eb and Gunner, who were sleeping away on the tiny speck of sand, they called an island.

"Hello? Kanek? You know what ignore my question, I don't care. The fact is we have a boat. Let's head for Lagos, on the coast of West Africa. Haines was reported to be there. So we must attend there. Small warning by the way, he's merciless, so do not mess around with him or his men. We do this my way. But since you helped me out of that dungeon they call a storage room, I will help you gain whatever it is that you need. So go on, what is it that you want?", asked Cain, appearing to share very minimal interest in whatever Kanek was about to say.

"Firstly, le's get som' mo' people on dis boat, so we can sail it. Yu stay here, and I'll go rally dem from my whaleboat. They're restin' on a small island, not far from here. Our paths cross since I wan' to return to my town of Imota with dem, and start a new life. I miss tha smell of tha tropics, and the warmth of tha air." This seemed to spark an idea in Cain's mind, as he stroked his stubble, with a weird grin on his face, chuckling to himself.

"Okay Kanek, here's what we'll do. We'll gather your people, and sail for Lagos. You help me kill those three bastards, and you can keep the ship, and I'll give you a good sum of money so that you guys can enjoy it amongst yourselves. Besides, killing these men ensures a safer future for all slaves. You on board with the idea?" Kanek hesitated to respond for a moment. He could still make it to Imota by boat eventually, and not worry about money or a ship. But a part of him wanted to ensure that his family got the best they could get out of life. What is liberation if you can't enjoy it? Thus, reluctantly he replied, "Ay, le's do it."

"That's what I like to hear. I'll deal with the captain, and look over the ship. You go surprise your family with this new present of ours. I'm sure we'll do very well trying to track down Haines down once we get there." Then Kanek remembered, and pulled out the dagger. Staring at the dragon sigil, he exclaimed calmly, "Don' worry, we've got a lead… " He showed the dagger to Cain, and continued to say, "He's gotta kno' somet'ing. I'm sure we'll find out somet'ing." Cain patted Kanek on the back, and made his way to the wheel to detain the captain, and to interrogate him to know more about the ship and what it contained.

Kanek made his way to the whaleboat and gently pushed off the side of the ship, so he could return to the island, to bring the good news to the rest. The sun was about to rise, and Kanek kept his eyes trained on the ship, as he rowed the boat back. There was something that seemed to bother Kanek. Something didn't feel right. But he believed deep down that he was just being really paranoid, and that Cain is offering him clear rewards. Even if he was to betray them, there was no way he could do anything about it. He was outnumbered. So with that thought, he rowed with more ease, knowing that nothing could go wrong, and if it does, he's prepared.

Thud! The boat had hit land, and Kanek sprang out to see everyone in tears, panicking. Except Gunner who was mocking the group. Azu approached Kanek, with a gaunt face, staring intimidatingly into his eyes, and Dara in the back, with tears rolling down her cheek. "What happun here? Why is everyon' cryin'? Who is responsible for all dis misery?", asked Kanek, as he stared specifically at Gunner, clenching his fist.

Ebenezer got up, grabbed Kanek by the neck and shovelled him into the ground, until Azu stopped him from punching Kanek and proceeded to say to look at the angry downed man, "Don't give him that look. We're like this because of you. Going off like that without telling us, and with the boat, we thought you had gone. The crates of food we packed in the boat is ruined too. Look at that. All that seawater has ruined it. I expected better from you."

Kanek rubbed his head while laughing quietly at everyone. "Wat is so funny? Knew yu were a bad idea," shouted Ebenezer, with a deep and hollow voice, cracking his knuckles. "I have somet'ing to make it up to yu guys. Don' worry too much, get in tha boat and I'll sho' yu. Maybe avoid tha takedown dis time, if yu can Eb", asserted Kanek. The group proceeded to look at each other, and then look at Kanek, with curiosity which dissipated the anger within them. But they decided to give him a chance, and entered the little boat, angry but intrigued. Azu stopped Kanek, and prompted him to sit down, and took the oars, staring angrily at him. "Aight keep headin' dat way, and yu will soon understand why I wasn't around when yu guys woke up," stated Kanek, as he signalled Azu where to go.

Azu began to row the boat away in the same direction, and the sun began to rise, and as the light lit up the masts and sails, everything became clear to the group. "A boat? But how? It's impossible, there's no way. You managed to secure a frigate? It's perfect! Judging by the size of it, I'm sure we can enjoy the luxury of sleeping on actual beds, assuming they have crew's quarters. But seriously how?,"shouted Azu in absolute felicity. "You crazy son of a bitch... ", whispered Gunner. They all started to murmur jovially amongst each other; smiles spread wide along their faces, except Gunner who still remained solemn.

"Well I was washin' myself off, an' I see somet'ing off in tha distance, so I decided t'take tha boat t'go see what it wa-" Kanek found himself interrupted by Cain who intervened by shouting down, "Blah, blah, blah, no one cares how Kanek, the point is that we managed to get a damn ship, and now we do as I say. Yea that's right, I'll take the wheel and control, and maybe we'll get things done." Gunner looked up at Cain and laughed. "Aren't you the little man that got captured, and tortured? Cain isn't it? The Order has done a number on you with his men hasn't he? Wait a minute, this is one of Haines' men ships." His face dropped, and there is a silent pause. "Kanek, leave him in there and let's row, we're better off in here than messing around with Haines." Kanek grabbed Gunner's coat, and shouted coldly at him, "Order of the Red Amphiptere. Sound fam'liar to yu?"

Gunner panicked, and tried to loosen Kanek's grip, and screamed, "Cain, you piece of scum, you told him about the Order!? They are the most fearless, insane men I have ever seen. They have no mercy, no compassion. Kanek, I'm telling you now, if you do this, we're both at a worse fate than death." Ebenezer replied, "I don' fear easily, I'll crush dere bones one by one if they touch us." Kanek pushed Gunner away, and neared the boat to the ladder, and proceeded to climb aboard, as he started to help everyone onto the ship.

"Cain, look ova here. I won' subject my fam'ly to anyt'ing less than yu. I do not work fo' yu. I am working wid yu. We ar' not slaves. We ar' humans. Do not tes' me Cain, you wouldn' be standin' freely if it wasn' for me. Respect us." Cain shoved Kanek away and took out his own sword, pointing it at him. Azu grabbed his machete and launched himself at him, while Kanek held him still, and told him to calm down and breath.

Ebenezer grinded his teeth, fists clenched, solid as steel. He prompted Cain to speak."You want to be respected huh? Lemme tell you something about respect then. Respect is given to those who need it. Those who earn it. And you disdain it! Now this is going to be *my* ship, so we are going to follow *my* rules, and you guys will do as *I* say. If you want control, you'll have to come and take it. Come on then Kanek! I'm right here!"

The air went cold, and there was a boiling mass of tension lurking in the atmosphere. Kanek prompted Azu and Ebenezer to stand their ground, and repress their rage, and Dara held back her tears, mouthing uninterpretable phrases, but evidently suggesting that the chaos must stop. They sheathed their weapons, and knelt, as they began to spectate. The two warriors started to move in circles, parallel to each other, swords in hand.

"I'm no' gonna kill yu, Cain. We need to do dis togetha," said Kanek, with hints of controlled desperation within his voice. Cain did not answer, and seemed to eye out Kanek, searching for an opening. He bit his lip sadistically and chuckled, and lunged forward with the sword. Kanek and Cain shared a parry, and their swords interlock in an iron grip, as they try to pry themselves off each other. "That all you good for? Being someone with no meaning, no respect, no penny to his name!?" whispered Cain into his ear.

Kanek felt a slow build of wrath; a scary, petrifying entity that ensnared his soul. His breaths were heavier, and his blood began to boil, and his muscles tensed up, hard as obsidian. "Coward, you don' kno' me! Yu wish to see what I'm capable of, then lemme sho' yu!" Kanek attempted to grab Cain, but he countered with a punch and threw Kanek to the floor and propelled him into a barrel, breaking it.

A bed of broken shards of wood and rusted nails proceeded to dig deep into Kanek's skin, tearing through his bandages, and causing him to bleed which incapacitated him. "That's all you got? I'm surprised you even contemplated defeating me. You seem to be bleeding away, how's it feeling? What a shame, looks like I'm gonna have to use you as an example, so that everyone knows me for the monster that I am. I'm a man driven by his goal, and you will not stand in my wa-" *Clink!* A bottle smash broke his speech, and as shards of glass began to sprinkle onto the floor, and Cain's eyes started to roll upwards as his eyelids slowly shut, and he fell to the ground, and there stood Gunner, with a broken bottle of rum in his bloodied hand, accompanied with unconcerned laughter.

"Christ, I couldn't have been the only one who was getting tired of his voice. Let's get outta here guys. I don't like any of you but I'd rather Kanek give orders round here, than listen to him for another second!" Using the railing as support, Kanek attempted to remove himself from the lattice of serrated metals and wood, but toppled over in front of Gunner, his blood dripping onto his boots, as he gripped his ankles. "Oh, will you get up, and go get yourself patched up. Dara you take him, go on. I'll deal with this skinny bastard by my feet."

Helping him up, Gunner unsheathed the dagger by Kanek's side, murmuring something to himself with a crooked smile. Dara latched onto the weakened Kanek, and aided him towards the crew's quarters, and Azu joined them, having shook Gunner's hand with strong gratification. "Well, I guess it's jus' me, yu and tha rat tha ground. I'll rope him to tha central mast. He'll be our guide back to Nigeria. Forget all dis nonsense about killin' men. We aren't mercenaries," exclaimed Eb, with a strong, deep tone. Gunner pivoted to Ebenezer, caressing the handle of his dagger, and walked towards him, patting his arms.

"And, you're damn well clever for doing so too. These aren't your men. They're twisted. It's bad enough Kanek has Garrett's sword. All of them have their own signature weapon. Cheval with his golden, heavy musket, and Haines with his rare, diamond spear, imported from Singapore. And Kanek has his sword. More reason to try avoid them altogether."

Eb laughed, and simply replied, "I'm not scared o'dem, but I do kno' they're not worth tha trouble." Gunner chuckled in response, and gave a warm smile of agreement, as he made his way to the storage room to talk to the captive, who was ironically the captain. Cain's eyes began to stir a little, his eyelids desperately trying to flicker open, while the rest of his body lay immobilized. Ebenezer waited patiently on a stool, unravelling a long rope, as the rat started to wake from its slumber.

Chapter 7: Unity

"May your choices reflect your hopes, and not your fears." **-Nelson Mandela**

"Let me out! Who are you?! Are my men safe? Answer m-*Arghhhh*!" Gunner stuck his dagger deep into the bottom of the captain's thigh, right above the knee, and twisted it around playfully, with the prominent urge to break open his kneecaps. "I ask the questions here scum!" said Gunner coldly, with empty eyes. "What's your name?" The captain put up a futile attempt of rebellion, spitting at him, and remained silent, as the blood began to run down his shins profusely. Gunner took the dagger out of the wound, and provided a momentary burst of hope.

But this was soon broken, as he slammed the blade back into the wound, and a tragic melody of sound proceeded to exit the squirming, defeated soldier, strapped to the chair. "Come on, work with me brother, I only asked for your name," muttered Gunner in a compassionate voice, with aggressive undertones, as seen while he fiddled with the dagger handle. "*Jacob*! My name's *Jacob*", he sputtered out miserably. "Jacob. That's a good name. Makes you sound a great idol. Now I want you to scream the co-ordinates of where we are, at the top of your lungs. I want you to scream so loud that you begin to feel your heart racing, as I drain the manliness out of that name, and everything you stand for."

Jacob remained quiet, his sweat and tears clinging to his skin, but the inevitability of the failure of his forced silence clung harder, but yet in a final stand of bravado, he followed through with his intended quiet. "We gonna play this game then? Fine I'll play along. Let's see how long it'll take to make you break!" The symphony of pain began to play out again, as Jacob tried desperately to avoid submitting to Gunner. "Do it you bastard! Scream!" The pain started to increase wildly, as the atmosphere hit a crescendo of melancholic intensity.

"I'd rather you waste your energy trying to find your answer, then tell you anything... ", murmured Jacob, with controlled anger. "What was that, Jacob, I can't hear you?!", jeered Gunner mockingly, and gave into his urge and popped off his kneecap. And just like Pandora's box, all of the locked evil and wrath spilled out in an angelic catharsis. "Arghhhh! Help! *Help!* Oh you son of a bitch, just wait until I'm out of these ropes, I'll ki-" The threats reached an abrupt halt, as a miniature waterfall began to surge vertically downwards from Jacob's neck, as the chair stood stationary in the middle of a wet, red circle.

Gunner felt relieved exiting the storage room, with the acknowledgement of the fact that his involvement against the Order (in being associated with these men who have commandeered the ship) was erased from reality. "That's how you tie up loose ends properly," said Gunner quietly to himself, as he made his way to the upper deck, wiping the warm blood off his dagger. He held a map in his hand with the correct coordinates circled in black ink, and laughed to himself, about Jacob's demise, and the pathetic bravado he put up trying to conceal information, when it was on his map all along. After the blood was rubbed off, the sigil is unveiled again, staring back at him. But he felt devoid of fear for a moment, but a new emotion. A mixture of light confidence and blood-lust, and in that moment, before he opened the door to the top deck of the ship, the thought of the Order of The Amphiptere did not intimidate him.

He felt ready to join a new crusade alongside his comrades, and felt an inexplicable power clasp onto him. The door opened and the cold, Atlantic air hit him and instantly, he felt every feeling of strength slip through his bloodstained hands, rendering him weak. "What was I thinking?" he muttered disappointingly, followed with a brief, deep sigh.

Gunner lifted his heavy eyes, and looked ahead, and witnessed Cain bound to the bottom of the mast of the ship, with a thick, braided rope, with an obvious exhaustion due to his lack of movement. "Now here's a sight for sore eyes!" exclaimed Gunner, with a splash of happiness in his countenance, as he advanced slowly towards him. He pulled an empty crate next to him, and proceeded to seat himself. "Lucky for you, your little friend downstairs had a map on him with everything we need to know to get to land, since we have the location right here!" sneered Gunner, waving the map in his face, as Cain stared at it with bland, uninterested eyes.

"So we won't be needing you as captain to lead us to our destination. Wasn't planning on letting you do anything. Scum." He spat at Cain jeeringly, and he reciprocated with a menacing smile, staring at Gunner's bloody hands, which seemed to shake Gunner for a moment, but he began to walk away. "You can't escape them Gunner. One way or another they will get to you, and they will find out what you guys have done. Kanek and everyone else will suffer no doubt. But you? You're a traitor. Betraying The Order, and harbouring these men, is worse than having someone who has no connection to these men do the same. They'll sear your soul in the foulest vats of hell. I hope you're ready to face that".

A gaunt, solemn look began to manifest in Gunner's face, as he stared at Cain with a concentrated ray of fear, and his skin scattered with crimson flushes. With a perceptible disinclination, Gunner stated brokenly, "You...don't know...what I'm capable of", and proceeded to storm off violently to the stern of the ship to join the paternal Azu, to salvage what little feeling of security he could.

"Come here Gunner, let me get a look at you. You seem rather odd today. Something about your face, you don't seem yourself," said Azu, signalling him to come closer, whilst stepping towards him simultaneously. "What's happened? You were fine when before you made your way to the storage room, and now you seem all serious. Not like you at all boy." Gunner forced out a reasonable smirk, with an almost visible curiosity sprawled across his face. "What's like me then?" laughed out Gunner, with his smirk developing into a smile, running his hand along the wheel.

"You know… the whole 'oh you guys are all scum' act that you try to put up, always getting on Kanek's bad side, you understand?" Azu noticed that Gunner had moved his interests to the wheel of the ship, and how firmly he gripped it as he stared off into the distance at the perpetuating body of water.

"You know we could go anywhere we wanted. The bright beaches of St. Vincent, in the Caribbeans, or even the grips of prosperity in England. That's the thing about this job, you see places. You breathe different airs, and explore different places. Never thought I'd end up here, splat bang in the middle of it all. And with people that I could have sworn I hated. I guess you guess aren't as bad as you're made out to be. Nothing that I can't get used to I suppose. Don't know about Kanek."

The words seemed to act as music to Azu's ears, as the delicate flesh of goodness arose from Gunner's shell. "We are family, Gunner. But if you can't decide where you want to go, your heart is not set on anything. But Kanek's one is. He saved us all and we owe him this. So it's Nigeria we head to. I'm sure you and Kanek will be fine. You guys aren't really that different," replied Azu, with a warm smile, and a solid pat on the back, as he left Gunner by the wheel, to tend to Kanek, Eb and Dara in the cabins. And soon enough, he was alone again, as the cold air hit his clothes in rising intensity, with only the fiery internal rage from the view of Cain, to heat himself, as he remained bound to the mast, keeping up his sinister smile and stare.

"You better stop looking at me or I'll severe those lips off your dirty face, and make you try to smile again!" shouted Gunner in an abrupt, aggressive burst of anger, clenching his fists. A roar of laughter arose from Cain, as his bloodshot eyes remained fixated on Gunner. "Oh, you're so blatantly scared that I'm embarrassed for you! *Christ*, just drop the act already! You think that you're above me, just because I'm down here starved, and you're up there by the wheel. You cannot escape the Order you moron! I want you to try to sail to the ends of this planet, and see if that fear diminishes. They will track you down and you'll be nothing but a pile of rotting meat to feed their hounds, you stupid, stupi-" In an uncontrollable vortex of wrath, Gunner grabbed his wheellock, and scrambled down the stairs towards the mast; the gun pointed at him.

"One more word. Just one and I swear to you, by God himself, there will be nothing stopping me from pulling this trigger. I don't know why you're alive, but I can tell you that I do not care if you die. But they think they need you, and I don't want to get on their bad side, so I'll leave it at that. But do *not* push me Cain." Although silence was achieved, Cain's cold smile remained in place, and haunted Gunner, as the pistol began to shake lightly in his hand, before he tucked it back in it's holster. "Good..."

There was an essence of thankfulness in his tone; a subtle vulnerability of the mind, and how even the thought of the Order left an unignorable, anxious expression on Gunner's face, and the empty surface of the ship had left him feeling nothing but bitter isolation. For the first time, he felt so alone, and it scared him; the thought of being the only one who will suffer the worst fate imaginable; a gruesome death by the powerful hands of the Order. He started to recite a mantra to himself.

"Fear the Order, Submit to the Bloody Three. Or the Red Amphiptere will find and murder thee"

All of a sudden, an epiphany had washed over Gunner, and he realised the complex predicament he was getting himself into, and how he must take a dangerous gamble. A 50/50 situation. Leave the ship, and abandon everyone, and hope the Order never find out about the death of Jacob and the commandeering of the vessel. Or to remain with his 'family', in the hope that he manages to seek out a way to escape the Order and that they never learn of his betrayal.

Gunner started to kneel in front of Cain, and gazed straight into his eyes, with an empty countenance. He reached deep into his pocket, and retrieved a sterling silver penny . "Call it Cain. Heads or Tails." A rush of bewilderment seemed to take control of Cain's face, and ironically, there was a sense of fear in Cain's eyes, whilst Gunner remained motionless, with coin resting on his thumbnail, ready for judgement by fate. "Why? What do I stand to gain if I call the right one." Gunner replied, "I won't ask you twice, Cain."

The air got colder, and the breeze moved the strands of brown hair that were in front of his eyes, exposing an intimidating and sharp blue eye. Gunner's patience seemed to wear thin, and so he flicked the coin, and watched the coin as it gravitated quickly onto the back of his hand, and in a flash, the coin is hidden. Gunner's eyes almost spoke for him, as if every word was oddly comprehensible from his murky blue irises, and how they urged Cain on to provide an answer. "Heads. I call heads," murmured Cain with intense worry, trying to control his volatile breathing, as if he were going to burst into hyperventilation. Gunner revealed the coin, and fate had chosen heads, just as Cain did. "I know what I must do now."

He got up, and there stood Kanek, with the others behind him, with an almost paternal smile, that provided a refreshing feeling of security, to which Gunner could do nothing but submit. He hobbled feebly towards Kanek, and held out his hand to his new brother. Kanek hesitated to reciprocate, but after having viewed the defeated, weak look in his eyes, he no longer saw the man who tried to take his life.

It was a petrified little boy, who chose him despite the risks. And just like that, two men of different ideals, were together and worked in union, in the act of a handshake, something that seemed unnatural to Cain. "You'll regret it Gunner, you'll regret this facade you're putting up. He's the enemy. I hope the Order tears you apart!" But the fear was no longer existent in Gunner, and he simply chuckled in response. "Are you mad! Do you see what you're doing! You're a disgrace. Where's your morals and principles?!" Gunner replied casually, "Look who's scared now." The union of the family was complete, and the elimination of the fear forever was next. The destruction of the Order, and the death of the *Bloody Three* had to be done, in order to eradicate that fear within him.

"Now we sail to Imota men! Kanek, you man the wheel, and Gunner, you keep control of the sails, and I'll aid you. Eb, I want you to take control of the cannons, so make sure they're loaded, and adequate for defences, and Dara, stand by Kanek, so he doesn't do anything stupid. No more of this Order! We have each other and that is all we need." An evident essence of dominance and certainty seemed to slide seamlessly off Azu's tongue, as the group began to take their posts in an obedient manner. Except Gunner who simply did not possess the capacity to tell them that the only way he could live with himself was to rid them of potential punishment and fear, by heading to Lagos, and shutting down the organisation forever.

But the words just did not form, and the joy in their eyes held a mental lock on his speech, and prohibited everything that Gunner desperately needed to let out. The truth lingered subtly, as he made his way to the ropes, to ready the sails for the vessel. Imota it was, and there was nothing he could do to prevent the fear-concentrated path he was set to walk. An endless avenue of bloody memories, and the balmy breaths of the Red Amphiptere condensing heavily on his neck. Gunner knew he was going to have to reveal his thoughts eventually, but he had no idea as to when, so that left him readying the sails. The journey to liberation was soon to begin, as the oceans presented a multitude of pathways and destinations, but Kanek's heart was set on one.

Chapter 8: Troubles Amongst Friends

The invigorating current of the Atlantic winds swarmed the surface of the frigate, as the homely vessel charged through the vastness of the glacial waters, with Kanek, who held the wheel with an iron grip, and Dara, who stood beside him with an air of untaintable loyalty. "How far are we from Imota, Kanek?" She interlocked her arms with his, leaning her head on his solid shoulder, as he stared off unknowingly into the distance, at the ocean. "I don' kno'. We are def'nitely goin' tha right way. Wen we see land, we'll dock, and all of dis will be put beh'nd us," whispered Kanek in response, as the blood-curdling memories of the tropical Imota, began to sprinkle doubts in his mind.

Was it worth facing the petrifying past, for a chance to initiate a beautiful future? But the warmth that radiated from Dara's cheek onto his stone-cold shoulders, and the way in which her fingers traced the outline of his chiselled hulk of muscle on his back, seemed to hurdle him closer to that dream. The vessel advanced through the fragile spheres of ice that floated innocently in the fluctuating waters, towards the coast of West Africa, and thus Imota.

Azu and Eb took control of the sails with precision, and ensured the wind had hit them efficiently, in the hopes they would arrive at the location faster, whilst Gunner sat on the crate by Cain, with an evident expression of contemplation, as time began to run out, the closer they got to Imota. "What's on your mind, Gunner? You look worried about something. Wouldn't happen to be The Order would it?"

The very words 'The Order' had his attention like a dog's when a tender slab of meat is flailed in front of it. "Just shut up. The Order won't know anything. I'll see to it that you remain quiet, and don't inform, and as long as we're in Imota and away from them, I'll be fine. One member won't mean much of a loss to their Order." But Cain didn't laugh. Instead, an almost pitiful look slid over his face, and the absence of Cain's incredulous chuckle disappointed Gunner, and in some manner, struck a sharp bolt of fright within him.

"Listen, I'm not going to pretend to like you Gunner. You're a bastard who works for that disgusting Order, and if they get more control of the slave trade industry, they'll be too rich for words, and can easily buy their way into power. Yh sure, Atlantic slave trade first, but what next? A power-hungry quest of control driven by uncountable riches?! They have men in every crevice of every country, an army, and you'll never escape them, especially when this ship docks, and they find out who the valiant helmsman and captain is. I'm not gonna tell you to do the right thing. But I'll say that escaping the Order is impossible, and your *only* rare, slight glimmer of hope is to destroy them three, so that The Order has no backbone, or a foundation to stand on."

Gunner held a writhing resentment towards every element about Cain, but a large, caged section within his heart knew that he was right, and that living in fear is not living at all. There would be no liberation. Only the psychological control of The Order. The metaphorical beast of The Red Amphiptere and it's flames of hellish fears. "Ah, you really are an annoying son of bitch, you know that Cain?" The lack of nourishment had exhausted Cain so much, that even a smile in reciprocation required too much of the nearly absent energy that he possessed. But Gunner knew what needed to be done.

And the truth was no longer going to be held back, so without hesitation, he lifted himself, with a steady stance, and strode confidently to the wheel, to break the repressed words that tried to dig relentlessly through his teeth. He took slow and calculated steps towards the helm, rehearsing how he was going to reveal it. But when he made it to the last step, there stood Kanek, and the pearl of the helmsman's eye, Dara.

The sun set to the side of them, creating a sharp eclipse of their bodies, as they began to form a natural, picturesque image of romance, that Gunner was soon to interrupt. He fumbled with his lucky coin, sliding it through his fingers, and squeezing it in his palm, trying to figure out how to initiate the conversation." Wat is it dat yu want, Gunner? Yu ar' beginning t'scare me." There was no evident expression of fright or fear in his eyes, but only a sense of curiosity and excitement, which seemed to arise from his hopes of positive news.

"There's something I need to tell you Kanek. Something I've struggled to tell myself, and come to terms with. Now, I have to tell you before it's too late." A dazing wave of confusion had stunned Gunner, as the words clung to his tongue like an adhesive. "Well? Wat is it? Don' waste my time, we hav' t'get there and I won' if yu ar' takin' dis long to tell me wat's on yur mind." Dara stood lingering at Kanek's side, sharing an equal curiosity in the words that seemed to have to be physically dragged out of Gunner's mouth. But there was no reason to hide it, so he wiped the moist surface of his forehead, and reluctantly replied, "We can't go Imota. Not yet Kanek." "What!? Why?" interjected Dara, as she subsequently looked to Kanek with bewilderment, and hopeful of answers.

"Yu he'rd her Gunner. Why is it dat yu wan' t'delay our plans?" There was a visible anger and assertiveness in his eyes, and it only seemed to increase as the seconds passed by, and as the sun descended under the horizon. "We need to kill them Kanek. We need to follow Cain, and kill them. The leaders of the Order." Kanek took a deep breath, and grabbed Gunner, and shoved him violently into the wheel. "He's gettin' in yur head Gunner. Yu don' listen to him, yu understand? Imota is so close and not'ing will prevent it. I'll kill dat bastard, I swear I wi-"

Gunner gripped his wrist before he could clutch his sword and storm towards the enervated man, which also abruptly halted his speech.

"It's not him, Kanek, it's us. We need to do this, or we're all in danger. And I don't know about you but I'd rather not live every moment of my life, peering over my shoulder, worrying if there's a knife there." Tears began to run down Dara's cheek, as her grip on Kanek tightened. There was a sustained lock in eye-contact between the two men, as their polarized emotions began to clash. Every word that Gunner said seemed to aggravate Kanek more and more, pushing him further away from their robust union.

"Why didn' yu tell us dis? Why did yu leave it t'now? Do yu understan' wat danga we ar' in cuz of yu. Yu hav' endangered all of us!" A feverish heat began to consume Gunner, as he struggled to maintain his composure. "I tried to tell you, I tried to tell you in the boat that we shouldn't have gotten on here, and that it was a bad idea, but ignored me, you ign-" Kanek struck Gunner relentlessly, causing him to stumble to the floor, as he burned in the bright flame of irrationality. "I told yu wat wuld happun if yu messed wid my fam'ly."

Gunner heaved himself up, and launched himself towards Kanek, as they both exchanged numerous punches and strikes, grappling with each other, with Dara, who desperately tried to separate the incandescent duo. "What is going on here!? Have you two lost your minds!?" bellowed Azu as he split up the two men, grasping onto Kanek with controlled strength, whilst Eb held down Gunner.

"Dat bastard got us into shit, an' I'm suppose t'be okay wid it. Now we hav' t'clear tha mess he got us in, if we're t'survive!" The rage seeped out of Gunner like molten iron, as every inch of his body was ready to finish Kanek. "Maybe, if you learned to shut up, and listen to others for once in your life, we wouldn't even be here you son of a bitch! Who do you think you are!? After everything, you still think you're above everyone here! You're nothing! You pile of shi-"

"That's enough! Look, I don't know what's happening here, but we need to start thinking practically rather than throwing insults at one another. Now, Kanek what's the plan? We sailing for Imota, or we listening to Gunner? Either way, we will support your decision." Kanek's eyes scanned around, as he started to think of the next step forward, and realised that there was only one thing he could do to ensure the safety of those he cared about. It was time for another suicidal plan. "Eb, untie Cain, an' get him to a bed. Get sum food in him. He's gonna lead tha way. I will help you kill dem Gunner. But afta dat, we ar' brothers no longa, yu understan'?" As Gunner's anger simmered, an unbearable weight of regret hung over him, as Kanek walked away with Eb to free Cain. "I'm sorry, Kanek. I'm so sorry..."

Pathos overwhelmed Azu to a point where he could not be irritated at him, as he sat by a miserable, vulnerable boy, in the body of a man, letting him lay in his arms like a child. "Hello, Kanek. You want a rematch? Or you just here to finish me off like a coward that you are? It's nice to see how much of an experienced captain you are. What was that fight? A brotherly tussle?" Kanek looked down at him in disgust, with a genuine want to kill him, and throw him overboard. But after having acknowledged his priorities, and how he wanted to ensure the safety of his family, he swallowed his pride, and retained his anger. "Get him outta tha rope, an' get him sum food befo' he dies on us."

As the clinching ropes unravelled and loosened, Cain experienced a strong incertitude, and was surprised at the supposed act of benevolence Kanek was carrying out, as Eb aided him up, and guided him to the quarters. An eldritch smile stayed stuck on Cain's face, as he walked away, with the ferocious shadow of Eb creeping behind. "It's settled den, we ar' goin' to set sail tomorro'. Tonight we rest men. Once Cain has com' to his senses, we shall go where he tells us." Dara came down the stairs, and to the central mast, and embraced Kanek, pulling him towards the crew's quarters. "I love yu, yu kno' dat." The words brightened up Dara's face even more, as she skipped towards the door, with Kanek following behind. "Oh, I love you too, Kanek." And whispered to herself, "I truly do." They disappeared into the compact interior of their valiant ship.

Gunner stood in utter solitude, after Azu left the stern to sleep. An impenetrable screen of tenebrosity and darkness slated over the sky, as he stared off into the ocean. The waters oscillated back and forth, and had an indirect, calming sensation towards him, as he found it easier to breathe. The grips of sleep did not seem to clasp him, and regret kept him awake, as he watched the thick clouds of vapour exit his mouth.

"Why are you so fucking difficult to work with!?" There was no echo, but only bitter silence, with the occasional soothing splash of the surrounding waters touching the ship's hull, to comfort him. He took out his bottle, that was refilled with rum, and began to drink, leaning woefully on the railing. The fuzzy feeling of intoxication and drunkenness crept upon him, and his sorrows seemed to disappear. "I don't need him. He's nothing special. If anything I pity that bastard! Me and him? Brothers!? What nonsense! When we hit land, I'm gonna kill all three of the leaders of that disgusting Order, and I'll see to it that I never make contact with him ever again. All of them!" And with that, he sat down, and he gulped down the rest of his rum, and fell into a drunken slumber on the stern.

Meanwhile, Kanek lingered in the darkness of his quarters, laying still on his bed, with the warm, sleeping body of Dara beside him. He lifted his eyes to the lantern that hung from the ceiling, and started to contemplate what he was planning to do. The very idea of taking on these three fearsome monsters of men, caused him to grip her tighter, as the loving heat from her chest filled that gaping hole of fear within him. The lantern stayed burning, and for the first time in a long while, Kanek truly understood the legitimate beauty of liberation, as he laid comfortably in his bed, with his lover by his side. The cold, trapping sensations of manacles did not haunt him anymore, and seemed a distant memory.

"Ah, wat a life I'll be livin' when I do dis last job. Kill dese men, and Imota it is. No more worries, no more Gunner. Jus' a small home in Imota, wid tha rest, a few goats, a dog, an' tha sun watchin' ova us." The vivid fantasies of the future gave him a profound mental stability that provided him the means of sleeping with nothing but jovial thoughts. But the subtle, destructive fear still remained, eating away at the back of his mind.

"Kanek, you awake?" Kanek fluttered his eyes open to find Azu by the door. "Wat is tha matta?" There was a brief silence. "Nothing. I just hope you'll find it in your heart to forgive Gunner by the morning. We have to work as a family, Kanek, not a team." A mocking chuckle escaped Kanek's mouth, as he replied, "He nea'ly destroy'd our plans. Now we ar' to try destroy three powaful men cuz he didn' inform us of tha dangerousness of dese men and how we were in trouble. He is far from fam'ly." Azu replied, "I don't agree with you, Kanek. That is not fair!" A savage and raw anger began to consume Kanek, coinciding with confusion. "*Wat!*" The sheer loudness of his response had woken Dara up, who was still tired and oblivious. "It's only because you can never let anyone get a word in! He told you to stay in the whaleboat and not to board, but you just never listen. You do your own thing and everyone else just has to follow along. Well it's about time you heard the tru-"

"Shut up ol' man!" The lantern had stopped burning, and the room was gloomy and quiet, and the heavy tension began to weigh down on them, and Azu's face had an expression of shock and upset. "If yu lov' him so much then go t'him. I do not care. We do dis my way, and dat's it. Me and Cain will be runnin' things from now on, an' once we're done. Gunner can go. And yu wid him if yu wan' to. Othawise, be quiet, an' leave my room!" Kanek reverted back to his comfort, as he laid in his bed, with Dara who was dead silent, and looking at Azu worryingly. "What happened to you, brother?", whispered Azu to himself as he shut the door, and went to his quarters. The ship was now silent, but the fiery tension still lurked around the frigate like a phantom, with hopes that the gaiety of the daylight will expel it from the vessel.

Chapter 9: The Journey

"Hell is empty and all the devils are here" **-The Tempest**
by *William Shakespeare*

Piercing shards of morning light splashed upon the boat, and Cain had forced himself up to acquaint it, and made his way to the kitchen. It was a delicate and rather small room, with a few barrels of biscuits, kegs of alcohol, and rotting fish insides on the chopping board. Cain seated himself, with a few crumbling almond biscuits in his hands, as he gorged on them, and tried to satisfy his endless hunger.

"Ah, my moment *will* come. The Order *will* pay for what they did to me. All three of those bastards. Now that I have these idiots, that shouldn't be too difficult." He chuckled uncontrollably at the thought of it, finishing his biscuits, and remained seated, thinking carefully about his plan. "Ay, Cain." He turned his back to find Kanek, who had just entered, with a cup in his hand, and an unconvincing grin branded on his lips. "Drink sum water, yu will need it for sure, afta all of tha time yu spent dere." He passed the mug of water to Cain, and sat opposite him on the round table.

"Why the sudden kindness. A few days ago, you would have liked nothing less than to see me rot away at the mast like a dying dog! A change of heart?" Kanek spent a little bit of time, calculating his answer, as the words were struggling to form in response. "Not exac'ly...I need yur help, and I know yu won' turn me down." This spiked up Cain's curiosity. "And what makes you think that now?" asked Cain, as he leaned closer, taking a sip of his water. "Cuz I'm afta tha Order. An' I know dat yu are too. So togetha we hope to destroy dem. Also, yu know dere location so yu are our only lead."

Cain finished his water, and slammed the mug into the table, and asserted, "If we are to do this, you have to be serious. From here on out, there's no turning back. We follow my plan and all of them *will* die. You have my word. I don't like you Kanek, but I'm willing to compromise, for the sake of killing them. Understand?" Kanek nodded, and shook his hand, sealing their deal. The bloody battle of The Red Amphiptere was soon to commence.

"Let's get to the helm. We must head to Badagry, east of Benin. Their organisation is based there, and that is where I intend to ensue chaos. We'll hit them where it hurts! And then you can go Imoga or whatever it's called, and hopefully never hear from them ever again." At this point, Kanek experienced the unignorable power of Cain, something he feared would happen, but he followed along to his orders, with the safety of his family at heart.

As they exited through the trapdoor, the two men were greeted with a medley of unfriendly faces as they moved to the stern. "Alright guys I'll keep it simple. There's a change of plan. We're going to the beautiful Badagry, where me and Kanek have some business to attend to." Cain nudged past Gunner, and helped himself to the wheel, signalling Azu and Eb to set the sails. "Why shuld we list'n to yu, rat?" sneered Eb, holding his ground, and holding his hand out, that hinted to Azu to do the same. Cain snatched away Kanek's pistol and screamed, "Because I'm the man with the *fucking* gun! Any more questions!? No?! Then do as I say, and set the damn sails!"

"Jus' list'n to him brotha." Eb looked to him abruptly and replied, "Don' eva call me dat. Yu two are jus' as bad as each otha. Yu can count on us to leave yur pat'etic self once we hit land." They moved to set the sails, as the wind began to pick up. "So much for not letting him get into your head. Come on Dara, let's go get something to eat." And just like that, Kanek was left isolated in Cain's impassable bubble of control, as he stood by him quietly, warming his hands. Gunner and Dara made their way to the kitchen, and Dara found a stash of vegetables in a crate, and some fish that was caught earlier that morning by Azu. "You wait for a bit Gunner, I'm gonna make us something to eat." Gunner sat patiently by the table, as she wiped the blood off the cleaver, ready to butcher the fish. "Don't be so hard on him Gunner, he's got a lot on his mind at the moment. He just needs some time to sort his mind out."

"Really? That's the problem? He's changed for the worst Dara. Surely even *you* can see that." Dara gave no reply, and continued to hack the fish into chunks, as she held back a tear. "I know you love him Dara. I've grown to love that bastard too. But something tells me that Cain is gonna ruin him." Dara stopped cutting, whacking the knife into the chopping board, and stared coldly at Gunner. "He just needs time. That's the truth."

They felt the ship begin to move, and the aura of anxiety began to corrupt the atmosphere, as they headed closer to Badagry. "And off we go. Dara, you need to see the truth for what it is, not what you want to see." He got up and advanced towards her, looking at her. "I know! Okay I know! There's a small part of me that knows that he'll never be joyful. No happiness. I know! I...know." She exploded into tears, overwhelmed by a hurricane of emotions as she submitted to the thoughts she swore untrue. Gunner gave her a hug, holding her as her tears slashed down his chest, and her miserable breaths melted on his neck.

"I just don't know what to do anymore... Everything has gone to shit." She lifted her tearful eyes to Gunner, and kissed him passionately on his lips. There was a mild reciprocation from Gunner, and time had slowed down, and he held her head carefully. Until reality hit. "We can't. What am I doing!?" said Gunner, nudging her away, processing what he had just done. They stared at each other emptily, and the words were trapped in their bodies, as were their thoughts. "Guys, we need more hands on deck, come help with the sails." They turned their heads in shock to find Azu and Eb who had just barged in. Gunner put up a nonchalant facade of obliviousness and ran to them, cueing Dara to do the same.

There was a mild consensus between them that hinted that it was never to be mentioned and that it never meant anything, so they stuck to that and went up the stairs, whilst the ghastly secret remained cemented in the kitchen. "What did he mean by 'so much for not letting him get in your head'. Is that what the fight was about? Whether to trust me or not?" Kanek peered at the new man at the helm next to him in awe, as he held the wheel with such care and precision, and how the vessel sliced finely through the body of water, nudging away the miniature icebergs. "Did you not hear me the first time, Kanek? It'd be damn nice if you knew how to provide any verbal response." Kanek was in a blissful daydream, which was broken by Cain's constant attempts at holding conversation. "Wat did yu ask agen?" asked Kanek unawares, trying desperately to remember.

"Never mind... Are you familiar with Badagry, Kanek?" Without giving him the opportunity to respond, Cain shouted, "It is the *heart* and *soul* of their Organisation, since most of the slaves are brought through that town, and it is a massive trading port. So make sure that when we get there, you stick by me. Because if you wander off or get caught, that's all on you. Me and Gunner *will* finish the job."

Kanek took a deep breath, and forced his weight upon the railing in front of him, observing his 'family' who seemed so distant from him, whilst being so physically close. "I've lost dem, havun' I?" Cain jabbed his arm playfully and responded, "Stop being such a soft imbecile! They'll come around soon enough. Especially that girl of yours, she sticks to you like glue!" Kanek let out a quiet, uncomfortable laugh, masking his misery.

"She's perfect. I wan' t'marry her in Imota afta all of dis." He began to wander back to his quarters, stretching out his arms in tiredness. He looked to the rest with hopes that they had forgiven him, but they simply carried on with their jobs. "I've got you right where I want you Kanek. No comfort. No hope. No family. Only me. You're my little puppet aren't you boy?", said Cain to himself quietly, witnessing Kanek's harmful rejection from the rest of his family.

Kanek entered his room and crouched by his bed, tugging out a crate of bottled rum beneath it. He whisked one bottle out of it, pulling off the lid, taking lengthy swigs, as the alcoholic fumes clung to him like a hook. Minutes passed by and the contents of the bottles emptied into the limitless portal of his stomach, as they clinked along the floor. His eyes began to view everything in hefty blurs, as his surroundings descended into a monochromatic mess. As the drunkenness pushed him into a sleep, he entered the realm of his dreams and imagination, providing him the crucial comfort he seeked.

"Imota! It hasn' changed a bit." He found himself relishing the soothing, vermillion afternoon sunlight, shining through the windows. The house was a mediocre one, with concrete walls, and with shredded paint on the side, whilst also providing the booming ambience of civility and goodness. "Kanek, come outside!" shouted a jovial unknown voice from outside. The voice helped him shift through the house to the entrance, whilst he held a cup of water in his hand.

He stared forward and witnessed nothing but the dreamy, orange strips of light that seemed to wrap around the soft, pink clouds. Kanek took his first step into the open, and felt the grass cushion his steps as he walked towards the lake in front of him. The delicate splashes of warmth on his skin kept him walking at a slower pace as he fully embraced the exotic land that was once lost to him. "Hurry up Kanek! Help me!" He turned his body and sped his pace, trying to locate the origin of the melodic voice, as it almost sang to him, until he reached a silhouette of a woman standing in the blinding light of the sun, with an unidentifiable object in her hands. "It's been a long time, Kanek… I was starting to think you had forgotten about little old me." Kanek approached the woman, squinting his eyes away from the light. Until they widened, and the figure was clear as day to him.

"Hello there Kanek. Miss me?" The very first love of his life, Daisy stood magnificently in the clean patch of grass by the lake, smiling at him, hiding something in her dress. "I don' kno' wat to say. How hav' yu been? There is much dat I wanted t'tell yu." She held his hand, and kissed him on the cheek, wrapping her arm in his. "Let's go for a walk Kanek. Let's make up for lost time!" They trudged through the grass, away from the lake towards a vast meadow, letting the soft breeze hit them. "I miss'd yu Daisy. I neva thought I wuld see yu agen." She skipped around him playfully, giggling like an innocent girl. She grabbed his arms and dragged him further into the field, and soon Kanek began to notice something.

"Yur skin, it's glowin' red!" Daisy did not seem to acknowledge Kanek's presence, as she continued to laugh and run around him. What seemed innocent at first seemed to go very twisted quickly, and Kanek wanted to momentarily extricate himself from her. He felt trapped in her fiery circle, as he kneeled down, clasping his ears, and shutting his eyes, trying to drown out her incredulous laughter, until she stopped in front of him. "Why are you so scared Kanek?" He opened his eyes to see nothing but crackling fires, as plants and the meadows around him started to incinerate.

He began to choke on the dusty air, and Daisy now looked different. "Don't trust everything you see!" Her irises were now blood-red, and her skin was crimson, with a few scales on her neck, and arms. Her teeth were sharp, with prominent canines, and she was no longer that pure woman he loved. "Welcome to hell, Kanek! My flames will *burn* you to ashes!" As he looked around worried, he saw an army of countless demons in hooded cloaks as they began to chant:

"Fear the Order, Submit to the Bloody Three. Or the Red Amphiptere will find and murder thee!"

The chants became increasingly louder, as his futile attempts of covering his ears did him no justice. Daisy approached him, as she grabbed the object she was hiding without revealing it, smiling crudely at him. And there it was. A pair of iron manacles dangling in her hands. "You'll always be nothing more than a slave! Because you'll always be trapped here." She tapped him on the side of the head, by the temple, to reiterate where he will suffer his eternal damnation. In his own mind.

The demons grabbed onto him, as Daisy forcefully placed the manacles over his wrists. "Why ar' yu doin' dis!?" The crowd began to roar with laughter, and she replied, "Because no matter how much you think you think you're liberated, no matter how far away you run, you can never ever escape who are, slave! Now hold on tight!" And in that moment, Daisy pushed him back, and Kanek found himself falling down a blackening abyss, with his hands wedged tightly in his manacles, until he hit the ground.

Kanek looked around and witnessed nothing but the sheer viscosity of the darkness that surrounded him. "Afta everyt'ing I dun for yu, yu betray me Kanek." Kanek peered, with tear-filled eyes, to find his mother standing solemnly in front of him. "Look at yu! Is dis my son!? Yu let me get captur'd by those men! Yu jus' sat dere! Yu-"

"Yu betray'd me! And father too. To t'ink dat I trust'd yu." Kanek remained kneeling, crying tears of both steaming anger and cold misery, and the sudden realisation of what he was, had hit him. The dull and rusted iron that held his wrists together reminded him. He was a slave and a prisoner, no matter where he went. "Son…"

"Son? *Son*? I trust'd yu, an' so wuld hav' father, but yu sleep wid dat man in secret? He is a pastor! Yu were betta than dis. Yu honoured yur wedding at one point an' now he is a distan' mem'ry to yu. So I don' feel like yur son." She touched his shoulder with a friendly maternal grip, and tried to extract as much sympathy from Kanek as she was physically capable of doing. But she was unsuccessful. The damage was done, and the transformation complete. Just like the iron manacles trapped his wrists, it trapped his spirit.

"Wake up Kanek!" A streak of pain remained embedded as a

headache in Kanek's head, as he straightened himself out, and seated himself on the bed, rubbing his eyes in an attempt to unblur his vision. "God, it stinks in here! Get up, we're here now." Kanek saw nothing but a sea of empty rum bottles, and Cain and Gunner standing disgusted at the sight of him. His body ached as he got up, and as Gunner helped him to the upper deck.

"Why tha change of heart, Gunner?"

"We all...do *things*...that we're not proud of, Kanek. And I guess I realised that today..."

Gunner realised that by pushing away Kanek for his lack of rational thought, he would

the quite possibly the most hypocritical man on that vessel. He would just be nothing less than a spiteful man. And as they opened the door to the surface of the ship, they saw the cluster of life that seemed to wash out of the docks in front of them.

"Welcome to Badagry *gentlemen!*"

Chapter 10: The Plan

Upon hearing those words, the sudden realisation had dawned on Kanek of how close he was to the end. There was no turning back now, and it was time to dissipate the terror that plagued the vessel, and to destroy The Order permanently. As his eyes started to readjust to the light, and his body to the blistering heat, he began to take in the beauty of the town. It was a thriving town covered in a small array of reasonably tall, yellow buildings, splashed on by the sunlight.

"Let's go. You guys keep yourselves quiet, I have someone to take care of you guys. Me and Kanek have some business to attend to. Gunner, you're gonna be with us too. I'll explain the plan on the way, so stick close to me and do exactly as I say." And the group began to set through the heavily crowded town of Badagry. They walked inconspicuously through various markets, nudging past noisy sellers, as they flailed products in their faces, and the rich scent of food submerged the market.

Cain lifted his hand to signal the group to stop, while he strode towards a man, greeting him with an excited handshake, who had an object in his hand wrapped in a silk cloth. He snuck a handful of coins into his palms. The man's face was thin and bony, and his physique seemed to resemble this too. He stood near a group of starved beggars lying against a wall, as he threw them a few coins. He was dark-skinned so Kanek assumed he was a native. He shot a smile at Kanek, to which he could only respond with an uncomfortable grin.

"What did he give you?" asked Gunner, trying to formulate an answer by making out the shape of the cloth. "All in good time Gunner, we're nearly there."

They took a swift turn towards an open door, and everybody followed Cain into the house. Cain walked on ahead into the house, telling them to wait where they were. Kanek looked around to find an average-looking living room, with a crackling fireplace, and a thin sheet of poorly woven threads for a carpet. In the far end of the room was a kitchen, of which he could make out a bowl of fruit on a table with a collection of flies buzzing above it, and a light vale of smoke edging out towards them. "I'm sorry that things got out of hand on the trip here, Kanek." Gunner reached out his hand apologetically, and saw some unexplainable guilt in his eyes. Reluctantly, Kanek shook his hand, but with confusion and not anger, as a proud Azu looked on, alongside a shuddering Dara.

"Why did y-"

"Guys, I'd like to introduce you to Mr Oza-*zey*? Am I pronouncing it right?"

"Mr Osaze"

"Yes Mr Osaze, he's gonna be taking care of you guys for a while. He's got somewhere for you guys to lay low. Take them round the back, we'll be back soon."

Mr Osaze was a man of a bulky build, with big arms and a prominent belly. He had a frothy beard, and was seemingly fond of the family, judging by his expressions. He exchanged handshakes with everyone, with a firm grip. "Follo' me." His voice was a hollow one, but his friendly facial expressions proved he was nothing like what his intimidating tone led him to believe. They walked further into the house and into the kitchen. He pulled up a large tapestry in the corner that revealed a hole in the wall. Kanek peered inside while Azu and the others walked in, and saw a staircase that led to multiple beds, and the soft orange glows of the fires that lit up the room. Mr Osaze passed Azu a bowl of fruit, and some water in a jar, to which Azu was grateful. "Thank you for your hospitality." He then undone the tapestry and that hole in the wall was no more. "My debt t'yu has been repaid, Cain. I will tak' care o'dem." Cain nodded his head with gratitude, and pulled at Gunner and Kanek to continue their journey.

"Your family is safe. Now before we commence the plan we must head to one market. I need to pull a lot of strings, and call in a lot of favors with a few of my friends in Badagry over my years here in the past, so don't muck it all up." Kanek and Gunner exchanged worried looks momentarily.

"So what *is* tha plan?"

Cain seemed to be irritated at the constant questions were shot at him, and simply just repeated, "All… in good time, Kanek", with a pause to emphasise his attempt of controlling an outburst. They walked past a horse that was dragging a carriage of 6/7 slaves, as they looked miserably at Kanek as he went past, with tears rolling down their neck.

"They aren't fortunate enough to walk freely on the streets. Lucky you Kanek. Auction must have happened an hour ago. Nearly there."

"Damn auctions. Tha worst feelin', standing dere, as they all watch, tryna buy yu, and yur just dere in manacles wid nothing to say or do. Until, one buys yu. Dat's it. Finished."

Gunner realised for a moment how much pain that Kanek had gone through, and this seemed to squeeze out every ounce of guilt that was left in his being. Did Dara lose his feelings for Kanek? Was it his fault? Should he tell him the truth? How would he react? Question after question began to shoot and stir in a mental stew, as he strung along with Cain and Kanek through a dense market, and the one thing that remained solid in his mind was that he would not be able to live with this guilt. It was just a matter of how he would break the truth to him.

"We're here!"

Gunner and Kanek aimed their eyes forward towards a small al-

cove of a shop, with swords and daggers hung on the inner walls as decorations, and an anvil in the centre. There was a small furnace on the back wall, giving off a bright glow and some orange, fiery sparks fluttering in the air near it, alongside an array of blackened tools. "How can I help you Cain?"
"I need you to replicate something properly for me."

Cain took out the object wrapped in silk cloth and placed it on the counter, and unravelled it, revealing a dagger. Gunner's eyes widened in surprise, as the sigil of The Red Amphiptere glistened off the metal blade. The blacksmith held the dagger delicately in his hands, holding it to eye level, as his face morphed into an expression of admiration. Cain swiped the silk cloth back into his pocket while the man stared lovingly into the dagger.
"Come back in a few hours. This will definitely take some time."
"Wait!"
The blacksmith looked back with a hint of annoyance, as if creating another dagger was a situation of urgency.
"I was hoping I could pay you for that with a favour. For old times sake. I simply don't have the money to afford that service. Come on, busy town like this, there must be some business you need taking care off."
He sighed in response disappointingly, but it seemed like as if it was something he expected Cain to say.
"How lucky are you that this is such a beautiful blade that I will work on this without a need for money. But business is business, so something needs to be done in return for this like you said. Head to back the way you came to the big market, and ask around until you can locate a man called Koyo. Tell him I sent you guys for that 'job' that needed doing. He should explain the rest."
"Thank you, we'll get straight to it. Be back when the job's finished."

Kanek gave brief goodbye wave, one that the blacksmith did not notice, due to his infatuation in the dagger. Gunner followed them around empty-mindedly, and oblivious to the situation, almost like a sad dog being dragged along by its owners. They made their way back into the thick crowd, as they began to somewhat interrogate the people around them, until the name Koyo became a part of the heavy chatter amongst the marketplace. They budged past countless people, asking stall after stall, but a similar set of monotonous replies were all they had gotten back in return. "Nope", "Sorry who?", or just a shake of the head.

"This is bloody hopeless! One man in this crowd, we'll never bloody find him. And we need to find him if we are to continue with the plan."

At this point, Kanek and Gunner had given up asking what the plan was, due to Cain's constant lack of an actual reasonable response, and the constant repeating of "All in good time." They walked around hopelessly for another 30 minutes checking every place they could find, but ultimately they were unsuccessful. On the way back to the blacksmith, as bearers of bad news, they witnessed a harsh confrontation between two men that became loud, spooking the passers-by.

"Yu told me dat tha money wuld be given today, but all dat yu hav' given is excuses! So it's abou' time I took back wat yu owe me, don' yu think?"

"Don' do dis Koyo please! I need it!"

And just by the utter mention of his name, their ears flared up, and approached him slowly. Koyo let loose a ferocious punch at the man, instantly dropping him to the ground, as he groaned in pain; his hands covering the spot of impact. He nabbed his bag, opening it, and grinning excitedly at the contents of it, as he felt the soft crinkles of notes inside.

"Koyo, we need to talk to you." Startled by the sound of his name, he shot through the men, in a desperate attempt to escape what he thought were guards, holding tightly onto the bag. "Afta him!" shouted Kanek, as he paced after the man instinctively, and Cain and Gunner followed. They began an intense pursuit through the town, slicing through a number of crowds, zooming through alleyways, and scaling rooftops. Koyo ran towards a ladder, making his way to the top and kicked the ladder down which denied all three access to the rooftop. In a second's worth of thinking, Kanek kicked open the door beside the ladder and ran through the home following Koyo under the roof, as Kanek kept his ears alert, trying to isolate the noise of his feet smacking against the roof. They made it to a concrete staircase that led to the rooftop, and managed to corner Koyo to a railing, where he could no longer run. The three men kept their distance to indicate that they were not threats, but Koyo remained worried, shuddering helplessly in front of the men. He pulled out a knife, holding it out as it wobbled in his grip, shouting, "Wat do yu guys wan' from me?! It was jus' business I swear! Don't come near me!"

"We... ar' not here... t'hurt yu man, we com'... wid good...intentions", said Kanek soothingly, trying to defuse the situation with his broken, tired voice, approaching him with gradual footsteps, and his hands hoisted up in the air.

"Oh...for Christ's...sake, will you drop...the damn knife! Samuel sent us...you know Samuel right? Said you had a...'job' of sorts...for us? Just...don't be so quick...to judge next time." A visible sense of relief washed over Koyo, as he flung his arm down, dropping the rusty knife on the floor. "I was t'inking yu were sum guards dat were chasin' me!" They all took a brief moment to regain their breath, and to restore their stamina, except Koyo who surprisingly still seemed stable and energetic. Once the heavy breathing of the men came to a halt, he proceeded to speak.

"Follo' me gentl'men, I'll explain on tha way", as he jogged softly to the staircase, clutching his bag, as the others stumbled along after him.

"Okay so dis job I assum' Samuel wants yu t'do is quite simple. He's a discreet man in dese areas, and sum people give him trouble. I'm sur' yu kno' he has a numba of 'side jobs', and certain people ar' revealing tha nature of dese businesses. Blackmailing him. I hav' a location, an' sum names. Kill dese men, threaten dem, do wat yu will, but make sure dey get tha message, and don' continue." Koyo handed Kanek a piece of scrunched up paper, with barely comprehensible writing jotted down on it, and did so in a manner that made him look ominous, as if the paper was strictly confidential.

"We'll ensure dat it will all go smoothly brotha, now get

you'self outta trouble and home." He nodded at them in response, and vanished into the open market like a ghost, and all they had to go on now, was a tight scrunched ball of paper. Cain snatched the ball of paper, undid it, and straightened it out to the best of his ability, and began to try and vocalize the scribbled contents within it:

"The...Fox's...Den I think is what it says." The name beneath seemed to be more legible, and read, "Jack Hemingway." Cain opened his satchel, and dumped the paper in there, as he swam through his mind, trying to think of possible places that the 'The Fox's Den' could be. Was it a shop, or house, or even an actual den, but nothing came to mind. "The name!", Gunner exclaimed. "That name... I know someone by that name. But what's he doing here? We're dealing with someone from back home, for me anyway. He must be here for some sort of financial gain, so I'm assuming most likely a gambling den of sorts. Somewhere where filth like him wallow, caring only about money. Know anyone who would know these kind of places?"

Cain took a moment to think, and evidently pleased with Gunner's theory, and scratched his stubble. "Mr Osaze", said Kanek. "Tha man has a damn secret room in his house, he'd kno' of places like dis."
Cain wanted to dispute this, but they had no other leads so he remained quiet and nodded, and headed back to the residence of Mr Osaze, with the hope of new information coming to light, so that they could proceed head to this place.

Chapter 11: A Friendly Favor

"The axe forgets; the tree remembers" - **An African proverb**

Noon had hit them, as the sun's light became less intensely bright and intrusive, and the heat was like a tropical tepid tenderness that clung to them, as they marched through the sandy streets. But guilt clung to Gunner just as hard, and walking back to Mr Osaze's house only catalysed it. The closer he was to Dara, and the more he had to witness her worried and anxious countenance, the harder it was to keep the secret. His heart ached for that explosive catharsis. *I kissed Dara, Kanek.* That was the sentence he repeated to himself in his mind. The words that would purge the fiery guilt in his chest. But was it worth the desecration of Kanek's tender and sincere emotions?

"I need a bloody drink", Gunner murmured carelessly to himself, as he lugged out a bottle from his bag and tried to empty the last of its strong contents into down his throat. "What the hell do you think you're doing!" bellowed Cain as he ripped the hard bottle and lid out of his hands, closed it, and chucked it in his satchel.
"Cain… Give me the bottle or I swear to God I'll-"
"You'll what? Hit me!? We have a job to do, and a plan to stick by, and I don't know about you but I'd like us to do that fully sober. So until this entire operation is over, you will do what I say and

the bottle stays with me. Really embrace the drops of rum left on your tongue, because you ain't getting this back for a while."

Gunner let out a solid din of an angry exhale in response, fists clenched, but Cain walked on, ignoring his display of obvious rage. There were more important matters at hand, and once that fact clicked in Gunner's head, he found his anger pointless, and continued to trudge along with the group, as a nightmare of passion drilled into his mind. Did he love Dara? Or was it just the guilt of betraying Kanek? The questions began to spiral into an aggressive whirlpool of ideas in the sea of his mind, breaking off the shells of sanity that clung to the sides. "We ar' nearly dere, I can see tha house." There was an odd smokey odour that oozed out of the building, and the closer they got, the more they could see clouds of smoke puff uncontrollably out of the building. "Shit!" shouted Gunner, as they paced down the street, as the crackling of the fire became more audible and clear.

As they made their way to the uneven shanks of burning wood by the entrance, they charged in the fiery, hellish domain that was once Mr Osaze's home, and found his body on the floor, alive and bleeding. He held tight on his wound near his solar plexus, lying flat on his back upon the heaps of ash, surrounded by metal plates and bowls, with bits of lukewarm food splattered aimlessly on the ground. "Kanek, get him out of the house, lay him to rest outside, keep him alive! I'm going to check on the others!" And just like that, Cain broke through the smokey, orange tinted interior of the house into the kitchen, coughing loudly, as his throat began to tighten, and his eyes sting and water.

Kanek and Gunner heaved his motionless body, as they held him from both sides, using his arms as leverage. His feet dragged along the floor, as the two men struggled to shift his weight out of the house. Once out, they kneeled, controlling their strength, as they laid Mr Osaze's nearly unconscious body to the floor. As Kanek took his hand of his body, a vivid patch of bright red blood stuck to his palm, with dark crimson lines of blood where his palm creases were. "Wat happun'!?", asked Kanek worryingly, as he repeatedly tapped Osaze's face to keep him alive and awake.

"Wat happun' brotha, we need to kno'!" Osaze's eyes began to roll in their sockets, as he tried to cling to every fibre of life in his body, gripping Kanek's wrists with profound intensity. Osaze fixated his eyes on Kanek, trying to open his mouth, and let his vocal chords run the words off his tongue. But he was only able to provide one. A name. One name. "Hem-ing...way". And immediately, he dropped dead on the spot, as the circle of red on his shirt became darker and wider, whilst the name struck chilling strums down their spines.
"Jack...Hemingway?".

They shifted their eyes at each other in silence and confusion, but equally in worry and panic. However, this was broken by the sharp load of coughs that greeted them, as Cain stumbled out of the hellhole. "Empty! Fucking empty!", repeated Cain in blatant disappointment, and noticed Osaze's bloodied corpse on the floor. "Whoever caused this fire, is definitely responsible for the poor bastard's death and the disappearance of the rest. So two damn things to deal with now!" Gunner crouched down and pulled Osaze's eyelids shut carefully, as he clenched his dagger with sorrow, and his breaths got heavier. There was an unsettling silence they held for him, as the building behind them grew into a fierce monster of a blaze, as the wooden fixtures sizzled and decayed.
"No Cain, we only have one problem now...", uttered Gunner through mental barricades of wrath.
"Only one..."
"How'd you mean?"
"Hemingway. He did dis. He has dem. And he's gonna suffa' fo' wat he's done today. *Vengeance is mine, I will repay*', says tha Lord. So I shall leave enough life in him for God t'set him on his path to damnation in hell. Dat is *if* my fam'ly are unhurt. If not, I shall take tha role of God, and damn him myself," said Kanek, standing with cold indignance in the light of the fire. And with that petrifying mental image of Kanek's full potential in regards to his strength and raw rage, Gunner realised how arduous it would be to break the truth to him. The dark, unutterable secret was the sacred key

that would unleash the 'vengeance' that he spoke of. So he remained quiet again. And swore to himself mentally to keep it.

"Well I didn't find the others *clearly* but I did find something Kanek. The fucker left a note behind. He knew we'd look in there. Hemingway will pay Kanek. We'll make sure of it along with the Order."

It was written on a decorated piece of canvas, trimmed to around 5 inches in width, with the words that read in blood, *'You have eyes but cannot see. They are blind to danger. They might lay peacefully. Like Christ in the manger... J.H.'* The note was flipped in the trembling hands of Cain, and there was a vivid red dragon that spiralled down the page, along with a secret message under it written in a code which he smiled to. Something that washed away all the tension that was bound to him. Gunner sneaked a glance, catching only the dragon, and immediately felt a piercing terror that bounced vigorously in the chambers of his heart. The Order had come to haunt them again.

"Well then, we're going to have to go through with my original plan. I'm assuming that's Jack Hemingway, and by the looks of it he seems to be working for that shithole of an organisation, so it's about time we get back to that blacksmith, and take that bastard down! We've got one shot at this. Let's make it count." Kanek remained kneeled and dead-silent by the soulless remains of a good man, as Cain stood with the enigmatic note stayed sealed in his grip.

    Cain placed his hand on Kanek's shoulder, to act as his cue to get up and join them, but he just shrugged them off with ease. It was as if every breath he took was controlled, as they pushed out tense, powerful shots of air from his nostrils, whilst his lips were quivering with rage.

"Yea. Le's go to tha blacksmith..."

The words seemed break and seep out of his clenched teeth, as he got up. Cain's grip of the letter was rising in intensity, as it crinkled and rested in his palm. They left, leaving Osaze's body lying drenched in his own blood, as the afternoon sun began to work its baking heat into his moist wounds. "We shouldn't have left him there. He deserved better than to rot there", murmured Gunner with a vague air of guilt. "Wat can we do? Dere are more important t'ings t'be focusin' on. Those animals hav' my fam'ly and they ar' my priority." Kanek's response seemed almost automatic. They walked at a more speedy pace, following the path back the way that they had came. Closer and closer to the stall. Cain's plan was set, and there was no turning back.

"Wake up Dara…" Dara forced open her sore eyelids and looked around. *'Where am I? Where are the others?'*, were the blood-curdling questions that raced through her mind. It was a dark room with patches of light sectioned off into different corners. Her sight was obscured by the darkness, and her ears were suffering from a repetitive ringing and subtle pain that wore down on them. She could taste a salty drizzle of blood from a cut on her bottom lip, and her hands were wetted by some damp spot of liquid that seemed to enter as miniature stream that trailed towards her from the door. *'I need to get out of here, and find the others'*, she thought worryingly to herself again.

"Dara… Help me…". Dara moved her head frantically trying to locate the fading, croaking voice, and managed to make out a silhouette of a man by the light in the corner of the room. She tried to get up to move towards it, but an abrupt piercing pain in her gut restricted her from getting up. She held one hand firmly on the area of pain, and used the other to crawl towards the figure. The closer she got, the damper the floor as the presence of light hit the reddish, thin snakes of blood that slithered towards her. And the sight had shocked her.

"Eb!" she gasped, as the burning pain by her torso prevented a louder reaction. Eb laid against the wall, with his massive hulk of arms suspended in chains above his head, and a constant dripping of blood descending from his mouth. His body was covered in purple lumps and long, vertical slices going down his centre mass that seemed bleed out infinitely. "We don'… hav' much time. Dey will be back. Pretend yu are… asleep. Don' get up… no matta wat yu hear… do yu understan'?" The difficulty that it took him to utter those words to her made her fear the worst. The horrid capabilities of these men.

Footsteps were subsequently heard, and a sharp jolt of anxiety began to juggle in her body, as she used up what precious time she had left to wipe away as much blood from his weary body as possible, before she scurried and slipped away towards her previous resting position, closing her eyelids tight. The steps got louder and bolder, until they arrived at a halt. A harrowing silence that encapsulated the room with a heavy feeling of doom. Her eyelids closed tighter, and her teeth ground together as the anticipation began to reel out the cold sensation of panic from her body. Her forehead was moistened with sweat as she lay motionless, waiting. For something. A sound. A voice.

The door swung open, crashing against the wall, and all Dara could hear was the slow and calculated steps of people walking in, dead silent. "Hello No Name... You still not gonna tell us? Let's try this again. Last time didn't go so well. My name's Haines", and he added semi-jovially, "And you?" All Dara could comprehend was the gentle but husky nature of his voice and how he sounded like a man of heightened respectability.

"Come on No Name, I'm not asking much. Just whisper it to me come on." He crouched down and held his hand up to get his guards to move out of hearing distance. "Look they can't hear you. Go on. Tell me." Eb lifted his head with a wearied neck, facing Haines. He was an old but well-built man, with a thick dark ginger beard and a trimmed moustache which sat on his top lip. His eyes were relaxing, like loops of brown honey, as the light caught his face perfectly. Eb remained silent.

"You know what? I don't need to know. I just need you to make a choice. Funny thing is... someone's gonna die. You, my friend, are just gonna tell me who", as a sinister smile arose from his face, as his head shifted to Dara. Haines sprung to his feet and clicked his fingers, as a guard stood alert. "Get my spear. It's time." Eb began to wriggle his legs away from Haines, as a guard hurried out of the room. "You've got a few minutes No Name. To think. And make a decision. Someone will die today. Someone here has got to take responsibility. I have eyes everywhere. And you think *I* didn't know about my ship docking. So for stealing my vessel, you will either die. Or... sit back watching her suffer the same demise."

Dara was still but tense as she tried with every effort to remain silent, and hold back her tears. The choice was clear, and a part of her wanted to take on the sacrifice. But the fear that kept her heart pounding wanted Eb to die. A horrendous but natural emotion that shook her. She remained still as the time was ticking and little hope was prominent. The guard burst back into the room with an exotic spear, with a red dragon that wrapped around the body of it, as the sharp tip gleamed in diamond.
"You have little time. I need an answer," said Haines as he grasped the handle, whilst keeping a stern glare at Eb, aching to kill. Sweat fell like raindrops from Eb's head, as a deadly quietude cursed the chamber with fear. "Fine, I'll take that expression as *kill the girl*. I must say I thought you were a gentleman. Clearly not... But if that's what needs to be done then that it is what will happen. The old man of yours is next."

Slow stepped and calm, Haines faced Dara and began to walk, as the soles of boots hitting the ground were the only audible noise in the room. Dara remained still, but her mind was far from it. Every possible perception of pain ran through her mind instantaneously. In what grotesque and twisted way was she to face her doom? The footsteps got louder, until they came to a halt, and all she could hear was the quiet breaths of Haines, as he towered over her; his spear in place. "You did this..." The spear was pulled back, and ready to tear through Dara's flesh on the side of her body, just under her arm.
"No! Kill me coward!"
Haines smiled at Eb as he looked back at him, who had nothing but hatred written in his eyes.
"So the man speaks! Very well. Maybe there's a gentleman in you after all...

Chapter 12: A Trip Down Memory Lane

<u>1632</u>

"You will regret this, Gunner..." The words clung to the man with fearful verisimilitude. He was to die by the hands of these men; these murderous monsters that evolved from normal people. Gunner was a youthful man, who lived with his family of three, which included himself. His mother had died from a serious case of tuberculosis, that had made her cough up blood, and rot away in her bed towards her demise.

His father and sister were who were left, lived in a compact little home alongside him. The interior was quaint with a small table covered with a red and white flannel tablecloth, and withering flowers in a jar in the middle of it. There were two rooms upstairs, where Gunner and his sister shared a room. His father, Dane and his sister, Stella were exhausted people, and had a thin and malnourished physiques, and they all lived, more or less, next to poverty.

Dane ran a stall in a nearby market selling his collection of aromatic flowers and shrubs, but he barely made enough to sustain the family. They fed off nothing but bread and cold meat every evening, and the monotonous nature of their dinner was essentially what starved them. They couldn't take it anymore. Something had to be done in order to resolve their situation. Not just the food, but their lives in general. It was too difficult.

The streets of England were riddled with injustice and gangs if looked at carefully enough, and essentially ruled over the markets. Extortions and threats were a regular occurrence, and soon enough Gunner found himself subject to this control, as he got dragged into a ruthless local gang, and exploited into doing illegal actions, and getting paid very little despite his efforts. This provided a temporary boost for his family, and they were able to afford to spend a little more than usual. Gunner's face became an infamous one amongst the town; a scary representation of evil that lurked within their crowd. The gang puppeteered him. Used him to keep away attention from the gang. A believable scapegoat. And they nearly created him into that 'murderous monster'; he was no longer the same person, and his family began to identify that.

"Where are you getting this money from Gunner!? No more silence do you hear! You tell me the truth now!" Gunner remained silent in his chair, as Dane slammed his angry fist into the table in rage, shaking the jar of flowers. The kitchen was silent, waiting for another explosive outburst from him. "I want an answer Gunner! All the sudden disappearances, all the claims I've been hearing from people!" Gunner did not utter a single word or syllable, and kept his eyes away from the heated glare of his father. Stella broke into a bundle of tears, as the anger intensified. "Everything I did Dad, I did for us. I couldn't care less about the 'claims' people are making! I want us to live well. To eat good food, to have a soft blanket to sleep under, and to even make you proud. I love you guys! Who cares where the money comes from!? What matters is that it's available to us!"

Dane began to rub his face with his palm in frustration, and gathered his thoughts as before he spoke again. "Are you...involved with those *wretches*... of a gang? Please tell me you're not. You wouldn't do that to us." Gunner's eyes dripped with guilty tears, as he looked to his father in desperation. His lack of response had explained it all. "Get out of my house... And never show your face to me again Gunner. You're not my son."

Gunner's eyes widened in despair, and Dane's eyes began to water as well, as he could not bear to look down at his broken boy. "No. We're going to talk about this! Please Dad!" There was a ripple in Gunner's voice as he spluttered out those words of hopelessness. Dane grabbed the jar of flowers and dashed it onto the floor, as the stems of the flowers were showered in their own petals, and the water leaked out onto the floor. He held Gunner tightly by the arm, dragging him towards the front door, screaming in his ear, "You are leaving my house, you pathetic excuse of man! I told you, day by day, never to associate with them! But you just didn't listen! You never listen! You-"

"Dad stop! We can help Gunner! Don't kick him out!" Stella's pleads were drowned out by the ceaseless rage that had ensnared Dane. He pulled open the front door, and shoved Gunner into the rain, as he toppled over and plummeted into a puddle as his father slammed the door in his face.

The rain fell heavily onto his head, as strands of hair fell over his forehead and stuck on. He looked with tragic eyes at that door, crawling towards it, and positioning his back against it. He laid there, resting his head and back against the wooden door, and closed his eyes, letting the rain cascade down his body and relax him. He needed the time to think and contemplate about how he was going to gain the trust back of his family. And then it hit him. It was his gang affiliation that had gotten him kicked out, so perhaps leaving them would be the first step towards gaining his acceptance again.

The next day, after having slept rough on the damp floor outside his home, he made his way to a block of old houses, that stuck near to each other like a long rectangular jigsaw, with the intention of ending his association with them, once and for all. He made his way to the second house in the row, the greyest of them all. The house was the quintessential haunted house, that gave off an eerie vibe as he got closer to it. He knocked on the door, fumbling with his fingers, and observing his surroundings. The house was on the verge of becoming a dilapidated wreck, with smoke exiting the windows, and the loud, heated muffle of voices just past the door. The voices then stopped and the door opened.

"Oi it's just Gunner boys, don't worry. No one to worry about." A bundle of mocking laughter arose as that statement was made. *'No one to worry about.'* The words poured a wave of vulnerability over him, and he came to realisation at that moment that he had no power in their domain. In that house of 'murderous monsters'. "I need to talk to James. Now." The men shot a bundle of smiles at each other, and then all simultaneously looked back to the shivering man. One nodded his head in the direction of an inconspicuous door, whilst taking a greedy sip of his cup of ale, signalling the men to guide him. There was a prevalent presence of smoke that arose from the door, as it tightened his throat. Two men of hulky build got up off their chairs in torn woolen clothes, and escorted him towards the door.

Gunner opened the door, and a cloud of smoke greeted him in return, causing his eyes to water instantly. "Where is this smoke coming from!" cried Gunner, accompanied with a number of aggressive coughs. The men said nothing in response and pushed his shoulder, forcing him down the staircase in front of him. Gunner placed his forearm over his mouth as he stepped down the stairs, trying to desperately peer through the smoke in front of him. The lower he went down the stairs, the thicker it became, until he hit the last of the steps. "Hello there Gunner! Don't mind the smoke, I've gotten used to it, you probably will too!", said James, as he walked forward, pushing away something with his other foot. A burnt, sizzling carcass of a man laid on the ground, as he bathed in ash.

"Is that..."

"A person? Yes it is, but he had it coming to him. We don't take kindly to traitors..." James put his arm around Gunner and strode away from the body, and deeper into the basement continuing his response. "You see for me, loyalty to our men, to our *gang* so to speak, is something I deeply treasure. I need that respect from everyone. And if anyone steps out of line… Well you saw that display. Anyway, what was it you needed to discuss brother? I'm just babbling on now."

Gunner's heart pumped vigorously, as the smokey stench that filled the room burst adrenaline through his veins. "I…want to leave, James." The words seemed to cut ferociously into James, as he waited with anxiety for a response. James grabbed him by the top of shirt, pushing him into a wall with hefty force and stared into his eyes solemnly.

"You want to what…?" Gunner fumbled with a series of possible responses that would hopefully defuse the situation. But he was limited to only one response that would actually answer the question. "I want to leave James. I gotta put my family first now. I can't be involved with this nonsense anymore!" James growled in hatred with every word that rolled out of his mouth, as the two henchmen stood behind him sharing equal rage.

"Nonsense! Is that what this is to you!" James hooked his stomach with a swift and solid punch, before he could utter a word, which dropped him on the spot. The air from Gunner' lungs shot out as he gasped, trying to catch his breath and clung onto his stomach. "Family yeah!? Yeah well I hope you're happy with your choice today. Get out of here!", and he continued saying the words that would haunt Gunner forever, "You will regret this Gunner…" He picked himself up, stumbling past the men in anguish, and to the staircase, tripping over the burnt corpse. His hands were covered in dusty ash, which he proceeded to rub off worryingly on his leg, and then worked his way up what seemed a mountain of a staircase.

Once he was in the main living room of the house where he was originally greeted into, a man forced him to sit down on a chair, with a cup of ale in his hand. "Drink it before you go. I could hear everything downstairs from here. Have a cup before you leave us." Gunner had nothing he could say to dispute the offer, especially since he couldn't risk taking another beating, or potentially fatal blow to the body. "Drink it," said the man with blatant enthusiasm. With reluctance, Gunner grasped the cup of ale and gulped it down rushingly, and headed towards the door. The first step towards acceptance was complete.

During his journey home, a burning sensation began to grip down onto his head. His pace began to slow down gradually as the pain increased, and as a rhythmic thumping of blood was audible to Gunner, in his head. His eyes struggled to remain open, and he fell to his knees in exhaustion. "What…was in…that drink…?", he murmured to himself, as darkness washed over his eyes, and he fell unconscious subsequently. His body laid quietly isolated in an alleyway, a mile away from home. And destruction was imminent.

Knock! Knock! The house was suddenly greeted with sound after a day of pure silence. Dane and Stella had been nothing but quiet, with the odd, awkward *'pass me the salt'* type phrases uttered to each other. *Knock! Knock!* The day was sunny and bright, with a steaming humidity that overcame the house. Dane rose from his chair, wiping away his sweat with his handkerchief. The knocking became irritatingly frequent, and increasingly louder. "This better not be Gunner, I've had just enough of that boy!" Dane opened the door in fury, but his ability to shout was stripped at the sight in front of him. Men with sharpened shivs and crooked smiles stood maliciously in front of him, peering into his eyes, turning the shivs around in their palms. "You Gunner's dad?" Dane smirked at the question. "Who the hell is Gunner?!", he shouted. "Dad! Don't listen to him; he's lying. Gunner's his son. What's happened to him!?" asked Stella with a strong touch of panic.

"Oh you stupid girl…"

Chapter 13: Loss

"These violent delights have violent ends and in their triumphs die, like fire and powder" **-Romeo and Juliet** by *William Shakespeare*

"Oh Eb! I didn't want this to happen!" cried Dara, holding onto his near mutilated corpse by the wall. The spear had fatally punctured Eb's body, and tore through his chest, his torso, and also his ribs, as he bled lifeless blood out onto the floor. She knelt on the floor as she held him in her maternal grace, feeling nothing but regret. *'I should have been the one to die by the hands of Haines'*, she thought to herself. She shook her head in disbelief and misery. Eb was gone. And he did not deserve his demise. Was his sacrifice worth it? "I'll kill him for what he's done. I swear to you Ebenezer. I will take his life away from him!"

"It's done! There's the dagger replica!", Cain shrieked in delight, as he stared on with interested eyes. He reached over the counter to grasp the object, but Samuel swiftly moved it back to his body, and away from him. "Is the deed done brother?" he asked with a strain on his face, almost as if he anticipated the following answer. "I need the dagger to help you. You gotta trust me on this one Samuel." Samuel didn't flinch, and remained attached to the blade. "I don't need to trust you with anything! No offence, but you're not exactly the most reliable person I met. Remember, that night we robbed Lord Davidson's manor!?" A suitable reason for why he should be trusted was immediately robbed from him by the mention of that memory.

"Listen, you got the money in the end didn't you!?"

"Yeah I did, after I spent 3 months in his basement, tortured by those bloodhounds for guards!"

Cain sighed defeatedly at the argument.

"Look, I'm sorry about that but you don't understand. To even get close to them, I need that dagger. Look at this."

Cain opened his satchel and retrieved the note, pointing distinctly at the initials and then to the dragon that was inscribed on the back. The dragon seemed to spook Samuel, as the light shone at the brown canvas, as the dragon lit up in a blossoming red. The dagger seemed almost welded to his palms, but Samuel gave in, and reluctantly handed over the prized item, as Cain placed the note back in his bag, and prised the dagger out of his hands. "You better get those bastards, Cain. I'm trusting you on this." Cain nodded and grabbed the second dagger off Samuel that was used to make the replica and headed away from the stall. "I have an idea as to where they might be. Follow me guys." Kanek and Gunner followed with utmost curiosity, as Cain sped forward with his mighty will. His attitude forced confidence into the two men, but it was not to last much longer. The foul mist of fate has ensnared them permanently, and everything they stood for was soon to be worth little.

1632

"Ah, my head..." Gunner groaned as he woke up with a piercing sharp migraine, and spat out an ounce of blood. His vision was heavily blurred and his skull ached with a subtle pain, as it lingered in his head as he walked. He was so deprived of energy that everything had to be thought and not spoken, since his voice dissipated into a helpless silence. His knees were frail as he used the wall next to him to elevate himself.

His voice was croaky but he could speak, and he was adjusting his senses to suit his surroundings. He stared at his own palms until he was able to focus on the creases without fault or strain, and wobbled out of the alleyway. "Gotta get back at home," he said to himself, holding the back of his head, and walking haphazardly out of the alley.

The pain did not cease, as his head suffered a frequent throbbing. As he walked past countless men, barging past them, the only people he could think about were his family. Stella had been Gunner's beloved gift for hope. A beacon of blossoming benevolence that he ran to when his mind was troubled.

She had a captivating way with words, that melted the dark thoughts out of his mind, and he knew more than anything, he could always rely on her to support him, even if Dane had been sucked into one of his violent fits of anger. Even as he trembled on the way back home, the thought of Stella trying to provide Dane with the crucial solace that he ached for, kept him confident that he was soon to be accepted back into his home. Maybe not with open arms, but anything would be better than the cruel rejection he was faced with before, as he was chucked out into the rain.

What the hell was in that drink? Gunner arrived at his avenue, and jogged down it swiftly until he managed to make it to his house. Something had spooked Gunner. The door was wide open and hardly a noise peeped out. Nothing but silence. Taking calm and cautionary steps, Gunner approached the door, pulling together and focusing all his senses before he entered. As he looked inside, he found a series of broken and tarnished furniture, as well as a streak of stained blood that dragged along the floor towards the dining table. The crunching of glass and the crackling of wood was heard as Gunner entered the room anxiously. What caught his eye was the remains of the flower pot, being exactly where it was. Even amongst the piles of broken items around him, that broken flower pot seemed the only thing in the room that seemed normal. "Dad!" No reply. "Stella!" No reply.

He reached for a kitchen knife and followed the trail of blood and it led to his room, with the door shut. Every inch of his being wanted to walk away and run out of the front door. But he wanted to make the right decision for once. The grip on his knife grew tighter, and the sweat ran like streams of water down his face. He raised the knife to eye level, and used his free hand to turn the door knob. All he needed to do was push it. And he did. The room was pitch black, exempt from a single candlelight that was on the side-table beside him. He grabbed it, and walked slowly, using his hand to guide him through the dark, and felt the wall he was facing for a lantern. The candle shook lightly in his hands, until he found it. He sheathed the knife and opened the little glass window, and lit the lantern.

A burst of fire spiralled inside it, illuminating the room, and when he stepped away from the front of it, it revealed the horrific secret that was concealed in the murky darkness. "Oh...Gunner..." The knife and dripping candle dropped instinctively from his hands, with the fall swiping out the flame. Gunner froze on the spot, with an unresponsiveness in his facial expressions demonstrated by his empty face. Then tears cradled his cheek as he looked down at his dead sister and his near-dead father who was looking at him dead in the eyes, and with such a firm conviction regarding his annoyance. "You know... I don't... even hate *you*. I just hate... what you become... A damned fool... Take this..." Dane moved his hand into his torn trouser pocket and held out a coin in his hand. A shiny silver sterling coin. "Take it... and run away. Before you're next... my son..."

And the light of his life extinguished there, as his head flopped back onto floorboard. Gunner held the coin with celestial strength, and used the other hand to shut Dane's eyelids. *Son.* Well that was it. Gunner dropped to his knees gripping Dane and Stella in his arms, as his tears washed away bits of blood that were blotted on their skin. "Thank you! Oh, thank you!" he screamed with infinite relief, and crippling sadness. He was able to get his father's acceptance back. But he was dead. They were dead. Gone to a beautiful realm that he was never to see for the daunting decades that remained of his life. He came seeking family and acceptance. And he was to leave with one of those things. A void that would never be filled in his heart and soul. Unless.

Revenge. I'm going to murder that bastard for what he's done. The blistering lava of revenge would fill that void and thus, liberate him from the shackles of pain and loss that were going to trap him. So he grabbed the knife from his waist, closed the bedroom door, and exited the room, stowing the knife on his waist. He kissed the coin with passion, and flipped it. *Heads or tails? Heads seems right.* He revealed the coin back to himself and there was the answer in black and white. An eye for an eye. *I'm going to kill you James.* Heads it was. And a head he was going to get…

Back to 1651

"Here it is men," said Cain with vivid excitement. "Dis is it? Yur sure?", asked Kanek with confusion. They stood in front of a cellar door behind an abandoned house with a sign of a worn-out, sepia shaded fox, with the lock broken off and placed on a barrel by the side. "Yes, I'm sure Kanek. You have your daggers men?" Kanek and Gunner held their daggers up in response to that question, and Cain nodded. "Good, let's begin then. You'll need them to gain access. They're essentially like a pass into their layer."

Cain concealed his face with a bandana-type cloth, and pulled out the dagger, opening the doors to the cellar. "You guys go first, I'll follow along." Gunner and Kanek nodded at him and then at each other, and unsheathed their daggers, making their way down the stairs. The pathway was moderately lit, predominantly darkness. "Keep going…" Cain whispered ominously into their ears. Something wasn't right.

A piercing wail was shooting through the corridor, with the miserable screams ricocheting and echoing through the pathway. Gunner and Kanek froze and stared at each other. "Why have you guys slowed down?" asked Cain uneasily, nudging him with his arm to continue moving. "Is dat Dara?" They stood silently, listening carefully to miserable pleads that were barely audible. *You…bastards…Ebenezer.* The words were broken but some seemed to shoot out at them. "Wait…Eb. He's here too!" Cain was getting heavily irritated and nudged them forward harder, and

Kanek turned around pushed Cain onto the floor. "Don' push me again! We need t'find dem."

"Bag them now!" It all happened in an instant, as two men with bags jumped out of the shadows, and threw the sacks aggressively over Kanek and Gunner's head, and with a deft of a punch from both the figures, both men were knocked unconscious and onto the floor. "Well then, I assume you found our note and deciphered the message then. Good job. You'll be rewarded nicely for your efforts. I knew payment would entice one of you guys here." Cain shook the man's hand, and walked back to his office for his reward. The unconscious bodies were dragged back towards a door that led to a cold cell, and they bound their arms onto the walls.

The cell was filled with darkness with two torches by the doorway that kept the room lit and provided mild strokes of warmth. Gunner woke up and jerked his head, accidentally hitting his head on the brick wall he was lying against. "Yu good brotha? I heard dat one." Kanek looked at the hurt Gunner who had been stripped to his vest, and still wearing trousers. "The bastard set us up! Just wait until we get out of these damn cuffs. Fuck, they're tight!"

"Yu'll get used to dem. I hav'. Yu kno'... of all tha people I'd end up wid in a cell, I wuld say dat yu ar' tha last person dat comes t'mind." Gunner stopped struggling with the chains and began to breathe. He needed to calm down, collect his thoughts, and most importantly not panic. "Hey listen, I'm sorry. For trying to fight you on that ship, all those days ago. I had a very... *rough* upbringing. None of this was part of my plan of how my life would pan out. I was doomed into this life Kanek." Kanek was confused. *'Doomed? He was doomed? Maybe there's more to him than I thought'*, Kanek thought to himself. "How did yu get involve' wid dese men Gunner. Dere's not'ing to hide anymo'." Gunner realised he was right. Neither of them had nothing to lose by telling the truth, so that's what he did.

<u>1632</u>

"I'm gonna kill him, I swear it to you, Stella and Dane!" he shouted into the coin, as it rolled back into his palm and was protected with a fist. "But first I need to get far away from this place. Somewhere that won't attract much attention. Get a plan ready. James will die by my hands, but I must think through how I will execute this plan. Before I execute him…" He made it down the road of his house, and glimpsed at the market. *Before I go, I gotta do this.* Gunner made his way into the dense market, and towards the Dane's stall. He went behind it, opened the drawer behind it with a key, and took out three aromatic flowers that were wrapped in linen.

They were dropped there by the man who provided Dane the flowers for his stall, an old family friend, and was to be sold for a higher price. Any longer and they would have been ruined. He ran back home, and into the remains of what was once his home, and found a white jar in the cabinet. He filled it with water, and placed the fragrant hydrangeas in it, and placed it on the table. "Had to give something to you guys before I leave for good…" And with that, he shut the door behind him, locked it and disembarked on his journey.

He marched through countless streets and crowds, and headed towards a series of slums near the Thames, where the rejected souls of society laid to rest and beg for their livelihood, and more importantly, it was a place where James' men would not think to look in. The stench that thrived there was near intolerable, and the families that lived there seemed to absorb the pity out of your being, but ultimately it was a safe haven for Gunner, free to stay, and gave him time to think and plan what he was to do.

He walked further down the street, and turned into a dead-end alleyway, with tired men and children aligned down both walls. He paced down it and found an empty spot to sit by the end, and rested his body amongst the filth of London. And he breathed. He was finally safe.

He closed his eyes, and almost fell asleep until it was interrupted by a threatening shriek of his name. "Gunner! You really thought you were safe didn't you!" Even before looking up to identify who the person was, his heart was pounding with excessive pace. "Oh you stupid boy! I'm sure you enjoyed the sight of what was at home for you! But it wouldn't be right to let you live. If we reunite you with them then you'll be happy again... Won't you?" He was followed. *Revenge. Revenge. Revenge.* His heart was no longer beating fear. It was beating anger. He ached for revenge. He could not live without it.

"I'll kill you, you son of a bitch!" screamed Gunner, as he took out his knife and charged at James, but his combat was simply too strong and fast, and was able to disarm Gunner, and kicked him with such blunt force that it dropped Gunner to the ground in agony. James kept him in place by applying pressure with his foot and took out a knife. "Listen here Gunner. I did not want this! You could have stayed. Get paid, support your family, and any problems with the law and we'd have sorted it for you. But no. You had to leave us. Like we didn't matter. So we had to take matters into our own hands. We had to teach you a lesson." James crouched above him, and raised his blade, ready to kill. "Goodnight Gunner, I'm about to set you free!"

Slash. Blood dripped down onto Gunner's face. And a groan of pain exited James' mouth as he dropped the cleaver onto the floor and fell in agony to floor. A man stood by Gunner's feet, and passed him a bloody dagger, smiling down at him. "Finish him. I can see it in your eyes. Do it. These people won't care." Gunner paused for a moment, but then snatched the dagger, and proceeded to plunge the dagger into James' chest repetitively, gaining more euphoria with every stab, until the man wrenched him off his corpse.

"Don't let the bloodlust consume you brother. Or you'll turn into him." That was something Gunner could not deny. *It's done my family. I've avenged you. He's dead.* Gunner shook the man's hand with relief. "Thank you. I don't think you realise quite how much you've helped me today. I will not forget this. I will repay this favour." The man smiled and replied, "My name's Hemingway. Jack Hemingway. And you?"

"Parsons. Gunner Parsons. Thanks for today. You've brought me peace in ways I cannot describe."

Jack nodded at him and was about to leave but stopped in his tracks. He pivoted on his heels and looked back at him with confident eyes. "About that favour... all of your anger and rage. It'd be good if you knew how to channel it. And you must not have anyone if you made the trouble of coming here." He flipped the dagger, wiping the blood of it. "Take it. I'm taking you to The Order of The Red Amphiptere. We will provide accommodation, training, food and all your needs, so long as you stay loyal to our cause, and fight alongside us, as well as a small sum paid every few months." Gunner found it ironic. *From one gang to another. How interesting is life?* But he was in no place to disagree, and had nowhere to go. So from that day on. He was a part of the Order of The Red Amphiptere. A man who had a purpose. A murderous monster.

Chapter 14: Cell-Mates

The story was finished, and Kanek felt a strong sensation of sadness for Gunner. Something he had not yet felt for him ever. To him, Gunner acted as a guide of the type of man you should never become, but in reality, his change in loyalty was something that was unquestionably admirable. "I'm sorry, Gunner. I can't imagin' how hard it must hav' been for yu." Gunner dismissed the subject with nothing more than a sigh, and a turn of his head. "After how long do you get used to having these cuffs on?" Kanek laughed faintly and responded, "When your mind is as trapped as your arms are... brother."

The door then burst open, and Cain, Haines and another man walked into the cell. "You fucking bastard Cain, you set us up! When I get out of these chains, I'll kill you!" Haines spun his spear with his arms as he approached the trapped men. "Hello Gunner. I don't believe we've met formally. I'm Haines. I'm sure you recognize the spear." Gunner's eyes were focused on Cain the whole time, but the gleam of Haines' spear and the sharpness of his eyes made Gunner silent. He was sitting in front of the big boss himself. The worst of the precipitators of evil that ran the Order. "We ar' not scared of yu. Do yur worst"

"Gunner, is that you?" Gunner swept his eyes away from Haines, and there stood a ghost of his past. " Wait, Jack! I remember you now!"

"What a touching reunion, but shame it won't last long. I have a surprise for you two. A choice for Gunner. And a verdict for Kanek. You two have been a threat to my plans for far too long, and it is about time I made an example of you guys. So that people understand who I am. *What* I am..." Kanek and Gunner swifty looked at each other, knowing that series of events that will unfold for them were only going to get more sinister.

I'm going to leave you falling down this maddening abyss with me. Kanek finally understood what Garrett meant. It was never the bloodlust. It was inescapability of their fates. Just as Garrett knew he was always going to be a pillaging, merciless demon, Kanek knew that nothing good would ever pan out well for him in this life.

"Do...yur...worst. Not'ing yu do can scare me." Haines was overcome with inquisitivity and immediately wanted to put Kanek to the test. "You think... I can't scare you?", asked Haines calmly, with a hint of underlying darkness. Gunner looked at Kanek and shook his head in worry. *Don't test him Kanek. He's crazy.* Kanek could read his expressions like a page of a book, but a major part of him wanted to see what was so cruel and fearsome about this man. "You're right. I can't scare you lad. Not without a little *pressure*. But it's fine. We'll add another pawn to the game. Bring him in Jack."

Jack took a brief bow and exited the room. Nothing had happened for five minutes, as Jack's footsteps became more and more quiet until it disappeared. The cell was quiet, and Cain's crooked smile had returned to haunt them once. Gunner had ran out of words to emphasise his hatred for the man. Every single fraction of his body wanted to break him, and make him try to smile through a fractured jaw and bleeding gums, but there was time for that soon. Hopefully. The footsteps began to start up again. Two sets of footsteps, and a series of indistinguishable pleads and sobs accompanied with it.

Who is that? Jack burst back into the cell, dragging Azu's weak body inside as he threw him to the floor, causing Azu to trip and fall, landing on his knees. "Azu! Listen yu don' touch him do yu understan'!"

"I don't think you are in any position to tell me what I can and can't do, Mr...?" Kanek said nothing, and in response to this silence, Haines smacked the back of Azu's head with such intensity that the sound echoed the cell. He held the spear just behind Azu's skull, and pulled it back with both hands, as if it were a cue stick. "Any last words old man? No? Well say good night..." Azu shut his eyes tight in fear, and when Kanek realised Haines was not bluffing, he shouted, "Agrinya! Kanek... Agrinya..." Haines put the spear in its holster on his back and clapped mockingly at Kanek.

"Now! Was that so hard Mr Agrinya!? Mind you, you are a hard nut to crack. But like I said. *Pressure*. Anything can be broken with the right amount of *pressure*." Jack dragged the sobbing old man back out of the cell. Kanek felt an almost animalistic, natural urge to kill Haines. Not a quick swipeL;';" of a sword, or pulling of a trigger. He wanted to hurt him, and watch the pain in his eyes, and feel the shudder in his body as he slowly passed away in front of his eyes. He wanted him to experience prolonged torture, and not be gifted with a sweet and painless taking of life. He too, had become a *murderous monster.*

"Well now. I'm gonna leave you two to wallow here for a while. If you need a piss or shit, just do it there, and hope you won't catch something. Remember. I've got a surprise for you both tomorrow. A very big surprise. So that should give you two something to think about while you're here. And I nabbed that sword from you Kanek, I won't even ask how you got a hold of it. Good day...", and continued to himself as he shut the door, "Wretches." The magnitude of Kanek's anger had reached his peak. His mind was forever changed. "Yu kno, I lost my parents too. My mother was takun away from me, and my father died when I was young. I still hav' nightmares abou' it to dis day."

Gunner tried well to change the subject, and hoped that the less it was mentioned, the easier it would be to deal with. But the truth was that it was something tragically embedded in his mind. The rum helped soothe the pain. But there was no rum. Just emotional turmoil. An hour had passed and Kanek had fallen asleep in his spot, and it had surprised Gunner how he was able to find comfort in a place as damp and eerie as that cell. And he started to cry in the cell. Everything had got to him. The past. The present. And the future. None of them had any element of goodness. No happy memories. Nothing worth remembering. And nothing good worth anticipating. The tears did not cease, and they were quiet, like gentle strums of sniffling that floated around the air. And eventually, the tears stopped, and Gunner had managed to fall asleep in his spot, resting his head lightly on the bricks he was stuck to, and shutting his eyes, as he let the wave of tiredness consume him.

Meanwhile, Azu was wide awake, as all of the anxiety and worries that came with his paternal mind fed the insomnia. His head was hurt, and his eyelids were aching to close, but he could not sleep, and breathed heavily. A sense of foreboding evil kept his senses alert. Jack sat in a chair opposite him, looking sternly at him. "Why aren't you asleep, old man?" Azu neglected the question entirely. Jack sighed and said, "Listen. I don't make the rules. Most of our members are here out of some sense of moral obligation. Gunner included. They give orders, I follow. That's just how it works. In return they pay for my family. My home. Everything. I had to make that sacrifice."
"Was it worth it? That man whose house you raided? You took his life! And you burnt his house down. You did that! You-"
"I did what I had to do! I was following orders. I have to block out my morality to survive. You think I'd still be here if I didn't? The Order has such a vast army. Haines, Garrett, Cheval, they are just the main leaders. They exist everywhere, with many officers running operations all over the world. This is not in my hands!"

Maybe Jack is a good man. Everything he does, he does for his family. Azu developed an understanding for why Jack was the man he was. He was simply a man who got dragged into the wrong crowd like all the others in that God-forsaken organisation. Azu could not see any reason to believe he was an evil man. If anything he felt that he was a victim. A poor, vulnerable man who could not live without the exploitative and controlling forces of men like Haines sustaining his life. Changing and altering his moral compass.

"Maybe, you're right. But an innocent man died by your hand, whether you were given a command or not. And that should tell you something. I understand it's not easy. But you can understand that what this 'Order' is, and everything it stands for... is completely wrong."

"I'm sorry old man. It's just... the way things are." Jack could not find any reason as to dispute that comment. Deep down, he knew Azu had an important point that he had to roll over in his mind. He killed an innocent man. He was so undeserving of his demise. Hearing that claim in words made him realise the full capacity of what he had become, and the guilt had hit him hard. He fumbled with his brandished dagger in his hand, as he thought deeply about himself. *'Is the real Jack still around?',* he contemplated.

The man who laughed and made corny jokes and puns with his daughter, as his wife looked both disgusted and amused at his humour. *Is he still here?* But one thing he knew was that nothing would change, and he would have to live out his life as it was set for him. Only death could save him from the cruel reality he was living in.

Chapter 15: Atonement

"There's nothing more calming in difficult moments, than knowing there's someone fighting with you." **-Mother Teresa**

Kanek and Gunner's consciousness of time was stripped away from them and this only heightened their anxiety. *A surprise. I wonder what it is.* After having woken up from their deep slumber, they relied on how tired they felt to try and figure out how long they had been asleep. "Listen, Gunner. Jus don' panic okay. Whateva it is, we will get thru' it."

Gunner believed in his words and nodded. They filled him with some confidence and managed to purge remnants of the anxiety that grew uncontrollably within him. Half an hour they spent, just thinking of all the possibilities of what could happen as soon as they left this cell. All the cruel and inhumane methods of punishments that Haines could provide. The rattling of keys was then heard, and the door began to open up slowly; the groans and creaking of the door hinges intensified as it turned.

Two guards walked in with bags in their hands and began to rummage loudly through their set of keys as they tried to find the right one. The cell was hot and musty, and when the shackles were free from their wrists, the guards threw the bags over their heads instantaneously. The starved men did not have the energy to fight back, and simply abided like mindless slaves to the control of those around them. *Oh God. I hope today goes well.* "Don't try anything clever. Now move with us!" Kanek and Gunner placed one foot in front of the other trying to coordinate and maneuver through the block of cells with nothing more than sound and the violent tugs of the guards as they forced them through every which way.

There was the brief sound of a door opening and they were subsequently pushed inside. The light from the room seemed to cut through the threads of the bag, and Kanek and Gunner were able to make out people, and a mild chatter amongst men. They were seated and the bags were taken off their heads. Haines and Cain were standing there, keeping wheellock pistols trained on both men. "Well, I didn't think it was fair to set you two on your big journey without a nice meal. Bet you boys must be hungry. Well here you go!" Cain grabbed two plates of aromatic food with cutlery, and placed them in front of the men. "Lamb's heart stew, with baby carrots and mashed potatoes. It's the best food you'll find around these parts that's for sure. Go on... Eat... "

At first they both hesitated, and just stared at the plate. Perhaps a futile attempt of a food strike might turn out fruitful. "Did you not hear me the first time? I said *eat* you bastards!", Haines screamed, banging his gun on the table, jiggling the plates. They grabbed the cutlery and began to feast on the food. The savoury richness of the gravy and the butteriness of the mash kept them gorging off the plate, as bit by bit the plate was getting cleaner, and all that could be heard in the end was the scraping of the knives and forks against their empty plates, with the miniature dunes of mash that soaked up the remaining gravy. *That was probably the best meal I've ever eaten.* When every last particle of food had vanished from the plate, they placed the dirty cutlery on the plates, and pushed in front of them.

"Damn you two really were hungry! Christ! Not a speck of food left on here. Should have let you out of that cell ages ago!" Cain and Haines roared with mocking laughter. "Yu kno' Cain brought us to Badagry t'kill yu. We weren' even headed here." Haines silenced the room and thus the laughter. "He did what?" Cain intervened and shouted, "Ignore him, he doesn't know what he's on about. I just searched the burning house out of curiosity and found that note. Then found them and brought them here! I promi-"

"Shut up! Continue Mr Agrinya... I wanna hear the rest." Kanek took a brief deep breath as Cain looked on with worrying but spiteful eyes. Gunner continued due to Kanek's hesitation and said, "He took me, Kanek and the others on the boat, and then here, then through town. He provided Kanek with a fake dagger replica to get close to you, but when he found the letter, he betrayed us. There was no coincidence. He wanted you dead. He still does! Ask the others if you want!" Haines tightened his fists and looked with malicious fury at Cain.

"Now. Cain. You have done me a great deed bringing them here. But I can't be sure that you won't come to haunt me and my plans again ." Cain's face dropped with panic, and Kanek and Gunner watched on curiously. "We had a deal. If I brought you these fuckers, and you set me loose with the cash. What's gotten into you!?" Haines moved his head and two more guards entered the room from behind him and held Cain in place. "You forget Cain. I make the rules here. Not you. Take him away. We'll deal with him later." Cain shouted out the most foul profanity in protest, trying to break out of the guards grips as they dragged the man noisily out of the room.

"Well done men. That won't save you two, but I'm sure you two must feel a little more relieved than before. Knowing that he will suffer. Get the chains back on them, men." The guards obliged and lifted them off their seats and put the manacles back onto their arms. They then placed the bags over their heads once more, and moved them down the corridor to the staircase, which led to the cellar doors.

"How will I get out of here?", whispered Dara to herself as she searched every nook and crevice of the room trying to find any structural weaknesses in the cell. It was sealed shut except for this one small, broken hole in the corner of the wall that let her look into the next cell. But the next cell was empty so it was a wasted feeling of salvation that filled her body. She stared through the hole for 15 minutes but nothing.

It was empty and devoid of all hope. Until the sound of keys jingling and mild muffled protests arose from the door. But it was not her door... She continued to peek through the hole, watching everything unfold, and witnessed Cain being dumped into the cell, and the door subsequently shutting. "Let me out of here! They are lying! Let me out now!" Dara was confused. *What the hell is Cain talking about!?*

"*Pssst*, Cain over here." Cain scanned the whole cell and found nothing, but the voice did not dissipate so he continued to search until he found a peeking eyeball trying to look into his cell. "I'm here. I'm here. Who are you?" Dara moved slightly away from the wall, and Cain managed to recognize her. "Dara!" Dara placed her fingers on her lips to silence him and proceeded to speak. "What are you doing here? What were you talking about? *'They are lying'*? What did you mean by that?" Cain scavenged quickly through a pack of lies that would help him escape the negative outcomes of that question.

"Oh I tried to tell them a false story about how we ended up in Benin. Kanek messed up the story in the process. But clearly it didn't go so well. Now Kanek is gonna get what's coming to him in about an hour. It was his own fault for not sticking to the story." Dara was immediately feeling the dangerous stings of worry and panic. *Get what's coming to him. What does that mean!?* She moved away from the hole and started to think carefully about how she could escape the cell. She had to think outside the box. Then an idea hit her. She ran to the door of her cell and knocked on it frantically hoping it would alert attention.

"What the bloody hell is going on with all that racket!"

"Open the door and come in. I'll tell you... *everything*," said Dara with a soothing, seductive voice as it sent tender, warm strokes down the guards body. The guard opened the door and closed it behind him as he entered the room, striding towards Dara. She came close, holding his jacket, and whispering sweet nothings into his ears. The guard grabbed her neck with force and pushed her into wall, kissing her with overwhelming force. Dara pretended to like it, using the kissing to buy time as she used her hands to carefully locate something. A blade or a blunt object. Just anything.

  She felt a handle underneath his coat, holstered on his waist, and every part of her told her that it was a blade. In a matter of seconds, she unsheathed the blade, and struck the guard by his obliques, covering his mouth with her hand, blocking out his screams. She pushed him onto the floor and continued to stab until she felt him stop struggling. And there lay his dying body, shuddering as he slowly lost blood. And a set of keys.

Kanek felt himself being pushed inside a cart of some sort, as the morning light that shone through the threads of the bag, disappeared as he entered it. The sound of horse hooves hitting and clunking against the ground and the creaking of wheels, told him that he was being transported somewhere. But he did not know where. There was nothing but the fear of the unknown that haunted him. Haines had him right where he wanted him. And Kanek had no choice but to sit there and imagine what sick, twisted plan he had in store for him that day. *Oh well, nothing we can do now.* The fear became less and less prominent in him, the more he accustomed himself to the fact that something bad was going to happen.

  The cart abruptly stopped and all that could be heard was a mass of jeering voices from the outside. The bag was pulled off his head and the guard whispered to him, "Welcome to hell lad!" The cart door was opened and there it was. It was all clear to him now. There stood the gallows from which he was to be plucked off the face of the Earth, in death. *Oh, so that was the damned surprise.* He stepped down and out of the wooden cart, guided by the guards as he walked on towards his peril. Gunner was standing there too, with visible fear as he shook mildly at the pressure of all these men. They were all members of the Order and the gallows were secluded not far from the abandoned house.

"Good morning gentlemen! I promised you guys entertainment so here it is!" The crowd began to increase in loudness, as the entire area filled with foreboding essence of death. Kanek walked up the stairs and stood next to Gunner as Haines began his speech. "Now men. Sorry about the absence of Cheval and Garrett. They are on important business ventures that cannot be halted. Nevertheless, these two men right here are an example of everything the Order teaches against! And as a result, they will act as a lesson to those who think of opposing me. Get the noose around Mr Agrinya's neck!"

The executioner, who wore authentic and thick robes, placed the noose around Kanek's neck tightening it, and placed a bag over his head. Kanek stood up straight, with his head held high. The fear of death was something he would not allow himself to succumb to. "Now remember Gunner. I said a verdict for your friend over here, but a choice for you. Now here's what's gonna happen. He's dying regardless. I will let *you* walk away right now. I'll open your manacles, and save you. So long as you return to the Order and remain loyal to us. Otherwise. I've got noose waiting for your neck too. If any of those men hurt you, I'll see to it that they suffer for doing so. So make your choice. And be quick with it."

Time froze for Gunner. *This is it.* He could walk away right now. Start again with the Order and there would be no repercussions. He would breath again for another day. Another year. Another decade. But the control, and the constant fear of the Order. *Was it a life worth living?* "Haines. Look in my pocket and take out the sterling coin." Haines was going to force him to make a decision but curiosity led to him to oblige to Gunner. He felt around and took out the coin.
"Now what?"
"Heads I live. Tails I don't"
Haines chuckled and without reluctance flipped the coin and slammed it back into his hands, concealing the outcome. "You

sure you don't want to just walk away Gunner?" Gunner shook his head, waiting on the answer. The final decision. "Alright then." He lifted his hand, and the gleaming coin shone the answer right back at him. "Well. Isn't that a hell of a thing." Gunner smiled and replied, "Yea, I guess it is." Judgement was finally made.

And there was no regret. No fear. "Send him to the gallows…" The noose tightened around Gunner's neck. He wasn't scared. Neither of them were. They closed their eyes. The lever was pulled. The crowd cheered. And two meaningful lives were washed away and forgotten in history forever. And poor Dara had arrived too late. The only tears that were shed in that vast crowd of merciless men, as she ran away. Now it was she who held a gaunt, solemn countenance.

EPILOGUE

1670

The hot sun beat on as she sat in the baking sands, tracing meaningless shapes into the grains of sand below her. The warmth trickled up her fingers, and she felt at ease. Nineteen years ago that day, two men of significant worth to her were stripped away from her forever. *I have to do it today. I have to.* Azu was never seen after that day. She did not even bother searching the cellars. She forgot. She genuinely forgot about the man that raised her. *He was probably dead anyway.* That's what she told herself. To comfort herself. But it was no day for comfort. The house was just over the sand dune. 3 days she travelled through that desert. And the end was finally within reach. She could feel it.

    She trudged her way up the sand dune, one foot after the other. And looked down to find a small quaint hut. Anyone would have thought it was abandoned. But she knew better. She skidded down the sand dune and walked over to the house. The door was already open. But then again who would be worried about someone stealing something from a house in the middle of a desert. She walked inside and it wasn't much. A petite chimney, a table and a charpai bed made of woven palm tree leaves that a man was laying on.

"Haines." He looked wan and pale, with a cross pendant on his neck. "Who's there?" She held back her tears as she approached the weakened man. "Nice place you have here... Nineteen years ago today... you took something away from me. People that I loved. And now... I'm here to repay the favour. It took me a long time to track you down. But now I'm here." Haines pointed to his cross and looked to her with eyes filled with regret. "I haven't got long left. I'm dying. I'm sure you can see that. I'm not the man I was before. I'm sorry. I understand if you don't forgive me."

Her face was empty and had a cold urgency to finish off Haines, and she simply replied, "I forgive you. But that's not going to stop the pain in my heart that I've bore for 19 years..." She took out her knife and plunged it into his body, as he let out quiet groans of pain. She slid out the knife from inside the wound and laid him down, as his blood dripped like tap water through the holes of his bed, and she closed his eyes. She removed his cross pendant and knelt beside him. Cradling the cross with bloodstained hands, she recited the Lord's prayer to herself. *I told you I'd do it Eb.*

The retribution was complete.

AUTHORS' NOTE:

I must briefly speak my mind about the journey that has led me here. Writing has always been a subtle enjoyment and outlet for me. The ability to be able to push my thoughts and emotions into words is simply soothing, and helps get at ease. I have been in many harsh and emotionally straining points within my life, and I have lost people who I loved dearly, who now live their own lives. Laughing and joyful. Writing this book has set that foundation for me to be able to live the same way. To enjoy life the same way, and I could not be happier. It has let me use my imagination in the purpose of entertaining others, whilst setting myself at ease.

I do not forget a single experience in my life. Nor do I forget my successes. Everything I do and everything that happens as a result of it will always be down to me, and everything I learn from those experiences is a lesson. This book is an accumulation of my dire thoughts and unorthodox imagination, and represents the bare minimum of what I aim to achieve in the future. To be a phenomenal author. And to make this happen, I must give thanks to the people that have gotten me here. If I do not do that then, I cannot hope to be a *good* author, but to simply bear the label 'author'. That is not respectable.

I'd like to thank my parents as they are the ones who are going to be investing into my book in regards to printing and mass promotion and are super supportive. I don't see my dream coming true without them.

I would also like to thank one of my best friends, Maisha Haque, for she was the one who sparked the journey of finishing this book. The messages of approval she had sent in response to my first and second draft filled me with the confidence required to be able to write this. If it wasn't for her, it would be another draft lying lightly upon others. I would also like to thank Reena Bhambi, my tutor, but she is more like family to me. Her facilities and belief in me kept me driven in the creation of this novella.

A massive, enormous thank you goes to Toni Cousins, my old English teacher. You might be wondering why she deserves this praise. But it is simply because she helped me develop this profound love for English. Not kicking me out of her class, despite my horrid behaviour, and poor grades. She believed in me, and as a result, English, a subject I once despised, is where I see myself at ease. So definitely a thank you to her. I would also like to thank people like Haris, Excel, Pirashanth, Zahra, Kajal, Mohini, Adila, and the list goes on for the people who have supported me and read my sample in completing this book. Without all of you, you would not be reading this in its entirety. Thank you.

Printed in Great Britain
by Amazon